BEYOND BEACHES

A COASTAL CAROLINA NOVEL

BY

DON GLANDER

Published by American Imaging
Cover design: Jim Grich
Format and packaging: Peggy Grich

Printed in the United States

ISBN   978-1-4675-7866-0

Beyond Beaches is purely a work of fiction. Though some dialogue, locations and characters are based on fact, the work is totally a product of the author's imagination.

ALSO BY DON GLANDER

BEYOND BORDERS

SET AGAINST THE BACKDROP OF THE ILLEGAL IMMIGRANT CRISIS, BEYOND BORDERS TAKES THE READER INTO A WORLD OF DANGEROUS TURNS WHERE THE SINISTER FORCES OF THE MEXICAN MAFIA AND THE SEEMINGLY PEACEFUL LIFESTYLE OF RETIREMENT ALONG THE CAROLINA COAST COLLIDE IN DRAMATIC FASHION.

"HOW ANYONE CAN WRITE A BOOK ABOUT ILLEGAL IMMIGRATION, MURDER, MARTINIS AND CRAB CAKES AND MAKE IT ALL WORK – AND WORK WELL IT DOES – IS AN INCREDIBLE FEAT."

MARK GORDON SMITH – AUTHOR
Tuscan Echoes: A Season in Italy

Trademarks

Anheuser-Bush
Barcardi
Bombay Sapphire
Budweiser
Cohiba
Coke
Google
Heineken
Igloo
Jack Daniels
Johnny Walker
Macy's
Marshall Field's
Martini-Rossi
Presidente
Sears
Yuengling
Ziplock

GRATITUDE

Once again it has proved true that writing, combined with the task of getting a book to market, goes well beyond the writer sitting alone with his muse knocking out a story, stuffing the manuscript into a folder, then sending it off for publication.

As with my first novel, *Beyond Borders*, there was help just about each step along the way in the writing of *Beyond Beaches*. Special thanks to author Jack DeGroot, *yet again*, for her first-rate edit and several significant suggestions. Thanks also to author Joan Leotta for her meaningful edit and to Bill and Sue Schwartz for their frank review. Of course the members of my writing group deserve many thanks for their candidness. Kim Shipman's cover photography is terrific, and thanks to Steve Veenker for his back cover insert. Sincere thanks to Mel Amos, Travis Elliott, John Heidtke, Chief Wally Layne, Rosemary Leonard and Bob Waskey, Barbara Lowell, Tom and Myrna McSwain, Chris Politis, Cindy Roach and Jackie Varnam for their special insights and contributions.

Lastly, my sincere thanks and appreciation to and for our Carolina coastal watermen. Through their hard work we, most fortunately, are able to enjoy fresh, local seafood. These folks are currently facing tough times as the result of rising operational costs, foreign competition (both legal and illegal), and government regulations and restrictions. Some of these men and women are fourth generation commercial fishermen. It is a heritage and culture from which we all benefit, and one we need to support and preserve.

Thank you all.

For Nydia

The center of my world
Approaching six decades

"Friendship is unnecessary, like philosophy,
like art...It has no survival value;
rather it is one of those things that
give value to survival"

C. S. Lewis

"Where we love is home,
home that our feet may leave,
but not our hearts."

Oliver Wendell Holmes

Each of us, when our days work is done,
Must seek our ideal,
whether it be love or pinochle,
or lobster a` la Newburg,
or the sweet silence of musty bookshelves.

O. Henry

BEYOND BEACHES

A COASTAL CAROLINA NOVEL

BY

DON GLANDER

PREFACE

Matt Paskins stretched his body over the port side and grasped the line connected to the bright, pink buoy with his left hand. He had to be quick. The strong current, combined with a substantial westerly wind made controlling the boat a very tricky business. The last thing Matt needed was for the boat to drift about and get the crab trap line wrapped around the engine prop. It had happened before. Leaning back and rapidly pulling the line hand-over-hand, he lifted the third trap off the bottom of the Intracoastal Waterway. Once free of the water, he grabbed the trap and slung it on top of the other two in the narrow space between the back seat and the stern of his Boston Whaler.

Taking a quick glance at all three, Matt guesstimated he had somewhere between three to four dozen keepers along with a couple of large stone crabs. He smiled. The stone crabs were a most welcome bonus; all in all, a very satisfying catch.

There were enough blue-claw crabs for several crab cakes, with a few left over to simply steam, pick and eat—accompanied quite naturally enough, by a couple of ice cold brews. The stone crabs, after removing the larger of the two claws, would be released back into the waterway where the claw, over time, would regenerate. Those claws, in Matt's humble opinion, were the closest things imaginable to lobster, his favorite food, and were worth the extra effort.

Matt's Whaler, *Crabby*, was forty years old, with an engine going on nine years, but she ran good, and people who know boats, which Matt didn't, had told him he owned a classic.

Matt began crabbing as a kid with his dad along the Jersey

Shore. Those were the chicken back-tied-to-a-string days. Crabs were caught one at a time, and each catch was an exciting experience, particularly for a kid. Once a crab was engrossed in munching away on the chicken back, it was carefully lifted toward the surface. A net was lowered into the water and slowly, ever so slowly, placed under the crab then quickly lifted, scooping the crab into the net. To miss, to watch the crab scamper off across the rim of the net and swim away, was about as big a disappointment as a kid could suffer.

He and Lindy built their place on Holden in the mid-eighties. Since then, using traps instead of a single string with a chicken back, he figured he'd caught, cooked and cleaned over 10,000 of the ferocious little beasts. Matt found that number hard to believe, but it was a fact. As he liked to tell folks, that's a ton of catching, a ton of cooking and a ton of cleaning, but also a ton of some of the finest eating known to man.

Not in any particular hurry, Matt ran *Crabby* slowly up the waterway toward the bridge connecting the island to the mainland. The bridge was quite spectacular. First timers crossing the bridge were often awestruck by the breathtaking, panoramic ocean view laid out before them. It was truly stunning. Rubber necking drivers were an on-going problem, and locals knew to keep their distance between them and the car in front when crossing the bridge. After so many years, and so many crossings, most island residents still never failed to be moved by the spectacular view.

This was the kind of day Matt savored, the kind of day that made retiring to Holden Beach the best decision he and Lindy had ever made.

Rain was in the forecast, but at this glorious moment there was a cloudless, Carolina blue sky, a touch of crispness in the air and to top it off, a nice catch on board *Crabby*. How could you beat that? It was a rhetorical question. You couldn't. It simply didn't get any better than this.

He slowly turned *Crabby* around at the bridge and headed back toward the inlet that would take him to his dock.

This was the way it was meant to be. Matt smiled to himself.

He and Lindy, just in the past week, had undergone a close call, a near death experience. That traumatic event had occurred on the stretch of the waterway where he and *Crabby* were now leisurely cruising. In one night, their relaxed, tranquil, admittedly enviable life, had become a nightmare. They were lucky to be alive.

Well, thank God, that's over, Matt thought as he turned *Crabby* into the inlet. *It's back to life as it was meant to be. Family, friends, books, music, preparing the occasional special meal, along with some great traveling thrown in, was what the good life was all about. We have our faith, and we have each other. What the hell, there will always be a few bumps along the way . . . that's life, but it simply doesn't get any better than this.*

There was no way for Matt to have known at that moment that nothing could have been farther from the truth. There would be more than "a few bumps." Much more.

And, as before, there would be no warning . . . the danger would be completely unforeseen.

CHAPTER 1

If you're in the Holden Beach area and possess a craving for fresh shrimp, some recently harvested clams or succulent oysters, a mess of feisty crabs, or possibly just some bright-eyed fresh fish, chances are you'll wind up at Captain Pete's Seafood, or one of the other fine, fresh fish houses near the beach.

On the other hand, if it's a nice day and you're in the mood to take a little spin, you might find your way over to Varnamtown and Garland's, known to many as Honey's Place, or one of its other quaint fish houses. But here's the deal on Varnamtown: you have to *know* how to get there.

Located a few miles around the corner from Holden Beach, in southeastern North Carolina, this small, picturesque, fishing village, nestled along the Lockwood Folly River, for some inexplicable reason, simply doesn't appear on some maps. In fact, a recently-published history of Brunswick County, the county where this village of fine, hard-working water folks, some of them third and fourth generation commercial fishermen, is located, neglects to even acknowledge Varnamtown's existence.

The thing is, from just about every aspect this anonymity is considered by most inhabitants to be somewhat of a blessing. The semi-seclusion that Varnamtown values, has protected their heritage and culture from much of the clutter and commercialism rampart in the world today.

Once acknowledged as the shrimp boat building capital of North Carolina, it has changed little over the years; the significant difference being that today there are few shrimp boats being built in Varnamtown. Construction costs are prohibitive, and the boat builders, the men who know how to ingeniously work the wood and design those unique vessels, many without use of a blueprint, or even a drawing, are now too old, or sadly, are no longer with us.

Aside from the waterfront with its aged, plank-wood docks and piers, and a few homes and house trailers along the river's edge, there are a few small residential neighborhoods, a convenience store, and three or four small churches—including the one obligatory to every southern town, Baptist. That's about it. No chain stores, hotels, motels, traffic lights, public bars or restaurants. And would you believe it . . . not even a gas station!

This suits the folks of Varnamtown just fine.

That is, most folks.

Inevitably, no matter how ideal things are, no matter that everything is going along just fine and dandy, there's always, *always,* someone who's gonna do his or her damnedest to screw things up.

Captain Mike Conrad guided *Naughty Nina* along the Holden Beach coastline heading east toward the Lockwood Folly Inlet. He was in no hurry. Spotting the large red and green buoys which would guide him through the inlet, he knew it would most likely be the last time he'd see them for awhile, and he wanted to savor these last few minutes on the water. The local shrimping season was about over and having decided not to work the more southern waters during the winter, they'd now be on the hill for several months.

He knew the police were already at the dock, giving him yet another reason to take his time going in. They were waiting for him and Willy.

Mike shot a quick glance over at Willy, his First Mate, who stood gazing off the bow of the old shrimp boat sipping a beer and enjoying a smoke. Willy was the only First Mate Mike had ever had. They'd gone to high school together, and after graduation, as Mike went off to college, Willy began working on Mike's dad's shrimp boat. After graduating from U.N.C., Mike returned to Varnamtown, wanting nothing more than to be with his dad and Willy and to become a shrimper.

They'd had an excellent haul for a three-day outing, and it felt good that the last catch of the season was a decent one. He hoped for Willy's sake, as well as for his own, that there were several more seasons left before the changes in the industry forced them to hang it up. Excessive maintenance costs, high fuel prices, pond-raised shrimp and imports from Asia, particularly Indonesia, Thailand and Ecuador, not to mention adverse government regulations, were already impacting the local industry. There were rumors that some of the shrimp processors were falsely labeling the imported shrimp as "domestic" or "local." Such practices, aside from being unlawful, had a dramatic impact on the livelihood of the local Carolina shrimpers.

On either side of the inlet separating Holden Beach from Oak Island, stood several surf-casters at water's edge, each harboring hopes of landing a few spots, a large flounder or possibly a couple of sea trout. You never knew which, particularly now in late fall, and that's what made it exciting.

There were children, and a few adults, in the water enjoying what would be, in all probability, their last dip of the year. The water was chilling down a little more each passing day.

Within minutes, Mike had passed through the inlet and taken a right turn into the Intracoastal Waterway. After a few hundred yards, he hung a left into the Lockwood Folly River, which would lead him to the Varnamtown docks, and home.

It was slow going from here on in as the channel was narrow and at mid-tide, left little room for error. Staring ahead, both hands firmly on the wheel, he tried to calculate the number of times he'd made this run since mating for his dad as a teenager back in the sixties. There was no way; he couldn't do it—he'd need a calculator. Mike grinned and slowly shook his head; *hell, it's gotta be somewhere in the thousands.*

The scene surrounding him had changed only slightly over the years. No matter the season, it remained as breath-takingly beautiful as the first time he'd made this run with his dad. There were the same wide open miles of salt marshes, with acre upon acre of sea grass carpeting the seemingly endless expanse. With winter coming on, it would turn golden, as golden as he imagined the wheat fields of Kansas to be. In the spring it would magically transform into a luxurious carpet of green.

Large, statuesque, blue herons stood, as they always had with their steely, yellow eyes penetrating the swiftly moving marsh waters with laser-like precision. Pristine white egrets perched upon the branches of what few bushes and scrub trees sporadically pierced their way through the sea grass. In the distant horizon, the gently swaying, still green marsh grass converged with the crisp blue, cloudless sky. *There's no place, absolutely no place, like it.*

As he continued on, the dozens of persistent, screeching sea gulls which had hovered around *Naughty* as she trawled the ocean, now followed her all the way in to her Varnamtown dock.

And then, and *then,* there was the aroma of this place. Mike inhaled, and again, more deeply a second time. It pierced his pores. He felt it travel to his bones. The aroma was part of him, and he, a part of it. If visual beauty lay at the heart of this area, then the sweet, pungent odor of the marshland was its soul.

Occasionally, when running these waters, Mike would

inexplicably experience a flashback to when he and Pam honeymooned in NYC—The Big Apple. It was the first time either had been there, and you could bet, their last. They'd been intimidated by the crowds, and were recipients of blistering headaches from the noise. Wasn't there a jack hammer pounding away at every intersection? They panicked more than once at having been rudely shoved about and separated briefly from one another. After the second horrific day they decided to hell with it, remained in their hotel room, ordered up room service, and did what they'd come to New York to do—honeymoon.

Negotiating *Naughty Nina* alongside the fish house dock, Mike saw the crew assembled to help unload, and the women who'd been called to head and sort the shrimp.

Except for the two uniformed cops, he'd known most of these people all his life. The women were the wives of other shrimpers, and oystermen, clammers and crabbers. They formed a tight community, with each member of this unique clique having been born and raised in or near Varnamtown and its waters.

Reflecting on New York again, he knew nothing like this could possibly exist in the north. It wasn't simply the physical beauty of this place that he loved, but the integrity, the culture, the heritage, the bonds and the uncompromising concern the people standing on the dock had for one another. Why so many millions chose to live in New York, and Mike figured most big cities were pretty much the same, was beyond him. Not when there were options. Not when Paradise did indeed exist elsewhere. He understood they simply didn't know any better, and that one thing was for certain, he and his friends weren't about to tell those sorry Yankees up north any differently. Or, as some of his friends might put it, sorry-*ass* Yankees.

"You got a smile on your face like you just landed a three-hundred-pound tuna, Captain," said Willy, coming up alongside him.

"I was just takin' all this in and thinking about those poor bastards up in New York. I wouldn't trade places with a one of 'em, not a single, solitary one—not for a million bucks, Willy."

"Well, I ain't never been there, but I seen enough on TV. Guess I shouldn't admit it, but I ain't never been outta North Carolina 'cept when we'd shrimp our way south durin' the winter. Remember, we'd dock in Georgia and Florida sometimes? Then of course, there was them few weeks running back and forth from Cuba during the boatlift with your dad. Them there trips was the sum, grandiose total of Willy Mitchell's world travels," he said with a chuckle.

"Believe me, Willy, you haven't missed a damn thing. There's nothing, absolutely nothing can top this," Mike said with a sweep of his hand.

"Hard to imagine anything could, Captain. I'm guessing you got things pretty much worked out in your head as to what you're gonna tell 'em," he said, tilting his beer can at the small piece of black cloth draped on the chair next to Mike.

As Mike pulled alongside the dock, he glanced over at the two policemen. "We're gonna tell them the truth, Willy. There's nothing to hide. We saw what we saw."

CHAPTER 2

Billy Bodean Dudley was, by every measurable standard, an S.O.B., and a first class one at that. Few have ever been accused of being second class in this regard, so if you're gonna be one, first class is about the only way to go. You could check with any Varnamtown resident, and he'd tell you that Billy Bodean sat in the front row of the S.O.B. Hall of Fame. If you didn't believe the locals, you could take the time to track down one, or all three, of his ex-wives. By the time you finished talkin' with those luckless ladies, you'd have the full skinny on Billy Bodean. But keep in mind you'd need to do some traveling as each former spouse had gotten as much distance between herself and her lyin', cheatin' conivin' ex-hubby as was sensible.

Foremost of his several despicable traits was that Billy Bodean had little, to *no* regard for the truth. Even if he tried his damndest, telling the truth for Billy Bodean would have been as rare as catching a marlin in Lake Michigan. If the truth smacked him along side the head, he'd wipe it off. If he tripped over it in a parking lot . . . well, the picture is clear. The man was, above all else, a compulsive liar.

Now that you're familiar with *what* he is, you need to understand *who* he is. First in this regard is: he's loaded. It's commonly acknowledged that Billy Bodean's the richest guy in Varnamtown. That may not be such a big deal in a town of five hundred inhabitants, but it's also understood he's one of the wealthiest men, if not *the* wealthiest, in all of Brunswick County, North Carolina.

No one knows for certain how his riches were first derived, nor how the seed money of his subsequent wealth first came about. But speculation runs high that it was the result of several illicit drug drops in the waters off the Carolina coast back in the eighties. The drugs, having originated in Mexico, somehow found their way into Billy Bodean's cigar-boat.

So, the big bucks follow right behind the lying part. Next up, no matter what the opinions of the man, a person had to give credit where credit is due. Using money from the alleged drug dealing, he bought land, and lots of it. That's another thing, he was a visionary, even back then. He bought land along the Lockwood Folly River, he bought land bordering the salt marshes of the Intracoastal Waterway, he bought land he knew could be developed into country clubs with multi-million dollar homes, he bought land he knew the county, state or feds would eventually want, and he bought it all at the right time and at the right price. Then he sat on it. When the coastal real estate market finally sky rocketed in southeastern North Carolina, Billy Bodean realized incredible gains of 500 to 1,000 percent, and more.

Now here's the last thing: if you weren't a resident of the area, if you didn't know Billy Bodean, he had this extraordinary talent for coming across as one of the nicest, friendliest, most sincere guys you'd ever care to meet. Some women, upon first meeting, even referred to him as *sweet.* He was, to his credit, a velvet-tongued charmer, or as one person who knew him well put it, a velvet-tongued *cobra.*

For example, say you and the family had driven down from Ohio or Indiana or New Jersey, having heard southeastern North Carolina had great weather, outstanding beaches, terrific sea food, and an abundance of world-class golf courses. Or maybe this was your third or fourth vacation in the area. You loved it and the kids thought it was terrific, but this time around you and the spouse experienced something different—a sudden, irrepressible urge to own a piece of this paradise. There would be talk amongst the family of Mom and Dad retiring here one day. After some serious financial chit-chat and a final reality check, you'd walk into Billy Bodean's modestly furnished real estate office in Varnamtown, express interest but inform him: "We're not really ready to buy, but we'd like to look around a bit."

He'd give you his best professional, friendly pitch and you'd shortly find yourselves in his red Cadillac Escalade taking a tour of his selected "choice" properties. By the time the tour concluded, chances were excellent that you'd seen something to die for and been "advised" by Billy Bodean to act quickly as the property was a real "steal." Since the kids had encouraged you to "go for it," in no time at all you shook hands and wrote an offer. The kids were excited and you and the spouse felt terrific about owning a little piece of paradise. One of the things that had you feeling so good was Billy Bodean's constant assurance that the purchase price was unquestionably a bargain; you had bought at exactly the right time. It would be later, perhaps years later, that you'd realize you had been screwed.

Billy Bodean might have sold you a house, or maybe just a lot, backing onto pristine marshland, assuring you that the marshland could never be built upon and therefore your spectacular view would never be obstructed. Or he might have told you that the land you were purchasing with that incredible view of the Lockwood Folly River would forever be unobstructed as the land bordering the river was owned by the Army Corps of Engineers. That awesome view would be forever yours to enjoy. Those assurances were unmitigated lies.

Such guarantees were never in writing and therefore appeared on no legal document. You, the buyer, had no recourse.

Such promises, for many, eventually led to shattered dreams, broken hearts, and sadly, in some instances, personal devastation.

Oh, there was one last thing that rounds out the picture of this low-life, and it should come as no surprise, Billy Bodean Dudley, admittedly through no fault of his own, and certainly much to his later regret, was mob connected.

CHAPTER 3

Matt pulled the Miata into the gravel parking lot of the Varnamtown fish house. The spiffy, red sports car was his wife Lindy's pride and joy. Well, that is, along with Satcha, their recently-acquired puppy. Matt figured he was running a close third at this point. But as for the car, she on occasion, always somewhat grudgingly and with a stern warning to be careful, permitted Matt to take the Miata for a spin.

Glancing around, he was puzzled to see Chief Curt Everhart's patrol car parked by the dock, its blue light flashing. A close friend of Matt's, the chief was seldom seen off the island during working hours, and Varnamtown was clearly not in Curt's jurisdiction.

A county sheriff's car was parked alongside that of the chief, its blue light also going at maximum rpm. Matt sat for a moment deciding if it was wise to walk in on whatever was going down. The desire for fresh shrimp, and the thought of returning home to Lindy sans those shrimp, trumped any indecision. He climbed out of the Miata and stood for a moment in the parking lot. Off to his left was Garland's, one of oldest and best known Varnamtown fish houses. He could see that the shrimp boat, *Naughty Nina*, was pulling in alongside the dock. Several people, including Curt and the sheriff, stood watching, waiting for her to tie up.

A short time earlier, Matt and Lindy had been enjoying late morning coffee while reading *The Brunswick Beacon* on their front porch, and saw the *Naughty Nina* slowly cruise by. Keeping an eye out for shrimp boats and other waterway traffic was a favorite pastime. Whether it was block long barges, porpoises, pelicans, gulls, egrets, or hawks on the hunt, there was invariably something of interest to be enjoyed.

But of all the sights, the thing that constantly astonished them were the yachts. They could only sit and shake their heads in wonderment as the parade of multi-million dollar vessels cruised on by in the spring, headed north, and in the fall, headed south. Matt and Lindy were doing okay financially, but the sheer number of people who owned those immense, gorgeous, sea-going ships was astounding. It was impossible to fathom so many people having that kind of money.

On this day, Matt, with Lindy's urging, had decided to be at the dock in Varnamtown when *Naughty* came in. The plan was to purchase several pounds of shrimp and stock up for the winter. Also, for years he'd wanted to watch the unloading and handling process. This seemed as good a time as any. He felt he had a decent chance with the crew of *Naughty* as he and Lindy had watched her go by their place many times. They usually waved to the crew, and on occasion, the crew of two returned their silent salutation.

❦

Matt, after surveying the scene, opened the passenger side of the Miata and removed a red and white igloo cooler. The cooler contained, in case it was necessary, a bribe of several cans of Anheuser-Busch's finest chilled hops and barley. He removed a second larger cooler in which to haul the hoped-for shrimp.

Coolers in hand, and with some apprehension, Matt made his way to the dock.

"What're you doing here?" the chief asked, surprised at seeing Matt standing at his side.

"I was gonna ask our top cop the same question. You've strayed a bit off the reservation chief. What's up?"

"Top cop, eh? You sucking up to me again?" Curt put his hands on his hips and looked straight at Matt. "Damn it Matt, did one of my guys ticket you again? How many times do I gotta tell ya, you have to slow down on Ocean Boulevard in that Miata! My guys see it and it's like waving a red flag in front of a bull!"

"No, no, no nothing like that. As I've told you many times, my admiration for those who serve, particularly those in law enforcement, and even more particularly for those on Holden Beach, is boundless."

The chief smiled and shook his head. "Now I *know* you're sucking up. I guess I'll find out why later. As it turns out, it's probably a good thing you're here. But again, you're here because—?"

"I was hoping to pick up some shrimp. But if I've walked into the middle of a dangerous shrimp bust, let me know. I wanna be gone before the lead, or the shrimp shells start flying."

"Afraid it's nothing quite so exciting," replied the chief, again grinning.

"Seriously Curt, what's happening?"

"We received a call from the boat's captain—said he'd found something we'd be interested in when they were trawling just off the beach—talked about a shirt—said he'd fill us in when they docked."

"Ah, man, come on, you should have called me right away! You know damn well it's probably—"

"I know, I know," interrupted the chief, shaking his head and holding up both hands. "You told me Delgado was wearing a black shirt, one of those Cuban things, the night he and his pal grabbed you guys. I was gonna call, but decided to check it out first. It could be nothing."

"Curt, you know I need to be there when you guys get with the captain. If what he found was Delgado's, man, it'd put that night of hell behind us, not to mention close the case for you. Carlos and Maria still have nightmares that Delgado is alive and on his way back to kill them. And get this, even though we *know* he's dead, Ché still appears in their nightmares. No matter what Lindy and I do to convince them it's over, they won't listen. But this will clinch it. It'll be over. By the way, it's a guayabera."

"What is?"

"The shirt."

"Oh yeah, I remember now."

"Well?"

"Now that you're here, I don't see—hang on a minute."

Matt watched as Curt worked his way over to the sheriff who stood at the dock's edge, watching *Naughty.* They chatted for a moment and Matt saw the sheriff nod his head.

Curt returned to Matt. "We're all set as soon as they tie up and begin off-loading the shrimp."

With *Naughty* secure, the women headed toward the fish house. The shrimp would be there shortly. Even though he had just received some tantalizing information, the shrimp process was part of what he had come for. Matt followed the women into the fish house. He figured he'd watch the ladies do their thing until Curt called him to meet with the captain.

There were seven women in all. They had stationed themselves around a long, large, white wooden table. As soon as a big bucket of shrimp was brought in, it was dumped in the center of the table and each lady, using an old auto license plate, raked in a small pile in front of her. They then began heading the shrimp. Surprised at how the heading was accomplished in one swift motion, Matt watched as one lady picked up a shrimp with each hand, pinched both heads off, then tossed the bodies into a bucket. The accumulated heads were scrapped into a narrow opening that ran along the inside edge of the table, dropping the heads into the marsh water that ran below the fish house, thus, Matt was certain, to the delight of the ravenous crab population frantically thrusting about underneath.

With some hesitation, Matt walked over to the heading table and stood by one of the ladies. She looked up, gave him a quick, curious, but not unfriendly look and continued working at a rapid pace. Feeling every bit the outsider, he gathered enough nerve to speak to her.

"Hi," he said.

"Hey," she replied, giving him a quick, sideways glance while continuing to pop shrimp heads.

"I've been watching for a couple of minutes, and really, I can't believe how fast you and the others are. How long you been doing this?"

"What's your name darlin'?" she asked, giving him another quick glance, but this time with a timid smile.

"Matt."

"Well, Matt, darlin,'" she drawled, "the truth be known, I can't hardly remember when I wasn't doing this."

Although everyone at the table was busy heading shrimp, Matt couldn't help but notice that the two of them had become the center of attention.

"My daddy was a shrimper, my husband's a shrimper, *his* daddy was a shrimper and my oldest boy first mates on my husband's boat."

"Wow, that's three generations—"

"Dolly, you can call me, Dolly," she said.

"Dolly, that's pretty amazing."

"Not really darlin,' you look around this table and it's pretty much the same story with each of us."

Matt saw the other ladies nodding their heads.

"Yup," Dolly continued, "we're just one big happy family."

"Maybe more like a tribe," one of the other woman laughed.

"A *lost* tribe," another snickered.

The ladies obviously enjoyed being in one another's company and appeared to appreciate the break in the routine.

Matt was struck by what he had just heard. It became clear to him that this was a generational thing—a generational business—a way of life that had changed but little, if at all, over generations. He hadn't considered it in that light. What he was now watching, what these ladies were now doing, was an integral part of an extraordinary generational craft. From the uniquely designed and constructed boats that roamed the sea and hunted down and caught the shrimp, to the simple but efficient layout of the fish house, all the way through to the process he was now observing, it was a different world. It had a culture and heritage far removed from the rapidly-changing, often chaotic, digital world that surrounded it. He had been transported back in time.

Matt stood, fascinated.

"You've got some really big shrimp there," he observed.

"Yeah, Mike had a good catch, lots of jumbos."

"You sort these by size, right?"

"Nah, we don't. That's Jimmy Irwin's job. That's him standin' over there waitin' for us to get him goin' with some shrimp. Hey Jimbo," she yelled over to him. "Get yourself over here."

Jimmy, a tall, tanned, lanky guy with weathered face, and a Lee Marvin look about him, strolled over to Matt and Dolly.

"Matt, this here is Jimmy. Jimmy's our chief sorter, he captained his own boat a while back," Dolly said.

"Nice to meet you Jimmy," Matt said.

The two men shook hands.

"You had your own boat?" asked Matt.

"Still do," said Jimmy, "The *Jolly Jan,* pretty ol' ship she is too. Still got her up on the hill. Just don't run her anymore."

"Where's the hill?" asked Matt, who couldn't think of

anything resembling a hill, or even a steep incline anywhere in the area.

"You're standing on it," said Jimmy, laughing. "Guess you don't spend much time on the water, Matt?"

"You could tell, huh? The only boating I do is dropping my crab traps in the waterway, and then hauling them back in. Sometimes we'll take a fun run to the Shallotte Inlet, or the Lockwood Folly Inlet, but I've never gone offshore. I'm afraid something will happen, ya know, like she'll stall out, and I'll find myself stranded and in serious trouble."

"I understand. Well, to answer your question, like I said, you're standin' on the hill. The hill is land. When you're out on the water, land is "the hill.""

"Ah," said Matt. "I've been living around here for several years and still can't believe how little I know. But Jimmy, you don't take *Jolly Jan* out any more?"

"'Fraid not. But sure wish I could."

"Why not?" Matt asked.

"Couldn't make enough money shrimpin' to keep her runnin'," Jimmy said, "simple as that. She'd already had a mess of years on her when I bought 'er. But even if I'd found a new boat, there's no way to make any money shrimpin', not nowadays. It got to where I couldn't keep fixin' 'er up and buyin' fuel, and payin' mates and what all. Not with shrimp prices being what they are. Couldn't afford to leave the dock. The upkeep and gas was just too much. Now I help out around here as best I can. But I'll tell ya straight, if this keeps up, there's gonna be more like me. You'd best take a good hard look around right now Matt, cause what you're seeing now ain't gonna be around much longer. I heard one of the gals, Sandy I think it was, just say we're a lost tribe. I know she was just jokin' and all, but I figure she ain't far from tellin' the truth."

"Well damn, Jimmy," Dolly interrupted, "if I knew you were gonna give a lecture on the sorry state of the shrimpin' business, I sure wouldn't have called you over! Who busted your britches today anyway? That was some kinda pep talk! Damn! Matt here was just askin' about the sortin,' that's all. No need for you to climb on your soap box and give the Gettysburg Address!"

"Sorry, it just gets to me every once in a while," he said. Jimmy looked around the heading table. Each of the ladies had stopped working. "Sorry," he repeated, looking down and shaking his head. "Guess I just miss being out there on the water chasing' shrimp."

The ladies had heard Jimmy's lament and that of other shrimpers, including their fathers, husbands and boyfriends, many times before, and knew he spoke the truth. The lifestyle and heritage their friends and families had lived for generations along the water was in jeopardy. But it hurt too much to think or talk about it. None of them wanted to give up, but each knew that the modern world, with its legal and illegal imports and hi-tech methods of operation, was closing in on them. It was just a matter of time, and not much time at that.

"I understand," said Matt, "I've been reading about the problems you're facing. It's something most folks don't realize or appreciate, or pay much attention to, and that's a shame. The shrimp you folks catch off our Carolina coast are incredible. To tell you straight up, Maine lobster used to be my favorite food in all the world, but not any more. I sure hope you're wrong Jimmy."

"That's for sure," said Dolly, shooting Jimmy a glance. "Now Jimbo, you fill Matt in about the sortin. I need to get back to work."

Jimmy examined the table where several buckets had by now been dumped, and the shrimp headed by the ladies. "I can pretty much tell just by looking as to what the count will be, but I weight 'em anyways just to make certain. *Jumbos* will run sixteen to thirty per pound, *Mediums* will run thirty-one to forty per pound and *Small,* forty-one to fifty per pound. Anything above fifty we consider bait shrimp around here. Although, I gotta tell ya, in some places there's even a ninety-one to a hundred count, can you imagine?"

Matt was looking over the table where there were now a mess of shrimp heads. "I keep forgetting what a large part of the body the head is," he said.

"Forty percent," Jimmy nodded, with authority.

"Now *that's* really a shame," laughed Matt.

"Well, ah, that's where their, ah, *intestines* are... in the head," said Dolly with a chuckle.

Matt frowned in confusion.

"Ya know, shrimp are where that expression 'shit for brains' comes from," piped up one of the ladies. Everyone laughed, even though they had most likely all heard it a hundred or more times. Fortunately, the remark lightened up the group's mood.

"I can sure see why," said Matt. "But how can you tell which—"

"Hey, Matt!" called Chief Everhart, waving Matt over to the office. "We're ready to get started with the captain."

Matt looked around at the group at the heading table. "Thanks ladies, and Jimmy. Nice meeting you all, and I really appreciate this. Gotta run, but hope you'll let me come back another time."

"Anytime darlin," said Dolly.

Matt walked over to the office. After he entered, the chief closed the door behind him. Looking around, Matt thought he had again stepped back in time. The office, such as it was, consisted of an ancient, scarred, wooden desk, four white, graying, plastic outdoor chairs, each with at least one broken or cracked slat. Atop an avocado-hued refrigerator sat a small, black and white TV with rabbit ears, tuned to a local weather report. There were two gray, rusted, metal filing cabinets. The adding machine was military green with a push button keyboard and a roll of printed paper with much of it curled over the side of the desk tumbling to the floor. The floor consisted of large, aged and uneven wooden planks, much as the flooring throughout the fish house.

"Matt Paskins, this here's Sheriff Veenker from the county sheriff's department, and this here's the captain of the boat that just came in, Mike Conrad, and this is his first mate, Willy."

The men all shook hands.

Looking over at the boat captain, Matt said, "You're not gonna believe this captain, but before we get started, I have to tell you that we sorta know each other."

"How's that?" asked Captain Mike.

"Every time we see *Naughty Nina* go by our place over on Holden Beach, my wife and I give you a wave."

"Good God," said Willy. "You must be the cocktail—" His face reddened and clamming up, he raised both hands over his mouth.

The Captain laughed. "Willy was about to say you must be the 'cocktail-hour couple.' That's what we call you two. When we go by your place in the late afternoon, you always raise your drinks and wave to us. So you're the 'cocktail-hour couple'—nice to finally meet you," he said smiling, and holding out his hand.

"Same here," said Matt, shaking hands again with the captain. "We've raised many a drink to each other over the last few years, ship to shore, or shore to ship."

"We have. Beer is all we keep on board, but we sorta always wondered what you two were drinking."

"Well, most of the time it's wine, but on occasion, when the mood strikes, we stir up a batch of Manhattans or, occasionally, I'll have a martini."

"Okay gents, listen, you two can chit chat later, let's see what we've got," interrupted the chief.

Captain Mike picked up a thin, plastic Food Lion grocery bag off the desk and handed it to the chief. The chief looked in the bag and removed a large patch of ragged, black cloth. He gave it a quick exam, shrugged his shoulders and handed it to Matt.

"Damn! This is it!" Matt said, holding the remains up for all to see. He couldn't contain his excitement. "See this stitching running down the length of the piece? That's how *guayaberas* are made. That's what he wore that night, a black *guayabera*! There's no question about it, it's gotta be Delgado's."

"You're sure?" asked the chief.

"Absolutely," replied Matt, grinning.

"Well, you're the one who should know," said the chief.

"Okay fellas, what, or who's Delgado, and what's going on here?" asked Captain Mike.

"First, why don't you tell us how you came across this?" said the sheriff, placing the remains back on the desk.

"Well, I have to tell you, Willy and I have seen a lot of nasty stuff happen on the water over the years, and like I said when we radioed in, we were just offshore finishing up for the day. We were headed for the Lockwood Folly Inlet when Willy here spotted something floating in the water," he said, pointing at the cloth. "The big difference being that when he first spotted it, somebody, or somebody's remains, was still wearing it. By the time we got into position to net whoever it was, a couple of sharks run up, grabbed the body, and ripped it apart. It was pretty brutal, in fact both of us had to turn our backs and stop watching. There was nothing we could do. You're looking at all that's left of the poor guy. After the sharks swam off we tried with the net for awhile, but there was nothing to bring back in except this piece of his shirt."

"Excuse me, Captain, but I gotta butt in," said Matt, picking the cloth back up off the desk. He held it up in front of him, smiled, and looked over at the captain. "I have to correct you on one thing. He wasn't a *poor guy,* he was one sorry bastard and this is the absolute perfect ending for him. My God, eaten by sharks! It's too good to be true!"

"Okay," said Mike, becoming irritated. "How about if somebody fills me and Willy in on what in the hell this is all about?"

"The best person to do that," said Chief Everhart, "is Matt here. It's his story. With your permission Captain, I'd like to take this piece of evidence with me." He placed the black cloth back into the bag. "Based on what Matt here just told us, and with what you and Willy saw Captain, we can wrap this one up. Delgado is dead."

"Clinches it for me," Veenker nodded in agreement.

"Not a problem, it's all yours. Glad it was of some use," said the captain.

With the departure of the lawmen, Matt lifted his cooler off the floor, placed it on the desk top, opened it and offered Mike and Willy a beer.

"Before we go any farther fellas, to be up front, this was intended as a bribe. If I arrive home without shrimp off of *Naughty*, yours truly could easily be the next shark bait you find floating out there. But honestly, after what's happened today, this beer is more for a celebration than a bribe!"

Captain Mike laughed as he popped the beer tab. "Not to worry Matt, we'll keep you out of trouble on the home front. I've had some experience along those lines myself. Now, fill Willy and me in on what the heck happened."

"Well, you guys just brought to a conclusion the most horrific event in my wife's and my lives."

Mike's eyes widened with curiosity. He took a sip of beer and looked over at Willy. "Guess we wanna hear this, right Willy?"

"I gotta little time on my hands this being our last run . . . got 'til next season the way I figure it," Willy laughed.

"Okay, here's the deal," continued Matt. "My wife does some interpreting work for the county and comes into contact with a lot of immigrants, some of whom are here illegally."

"Well, I can't tell an illegal from a legal, but I see what looks like immigrants all over the place, that's for sure," said Mike. "There's not a construction site, landscaping site, farm, or whatever, that doesn't look like most of the workers came from someplace else. Of course, that doesn't mean they are all here illegally."

"Well, no one knows the real number, but some guess we have about 500,000 illegals just here in North Carolina," said Matt. "could be more, could be less. But whatever, it's a pretty big number."

"Anyway, through her interpreting work, my wife, her name is Lindy, got to know this one pregnant, illegal gal who had run into trouble with the Mafia, the Mexican Mafia."

"Whoa! Hold on a minute. The Mexican Mafia? There's a Mexican Mafia? Here?" asked Mike, with a look of shock on his face.

"There is, and it operates here in Brunswick County, but believe me Captain, that's a whole other story," said Matt, reaching in for another beer. "Please, help yourselves fellas."

"Hey Matt, now that we're getting to know each other, the name's Mike. It's only 'Captain' on board *Naughty*."

"Okay. Thanks. Anyway, Lindy became friends with one of the illegal ladies who was pregnant. To be honest with you, there are many of these folks you feel sorry for and want to help. They've had a pretty rough time of it. Of course, there are also those who simply want to take advantage of the system. Anyway, this pregnant gal and her husband, at Lindy's doing, wound up hiding from the Mafia at our place over on Holden Beach."

"Why there? Why not go to the police?" asked Mike.

"Being illegal, it could have created some real problems for them," said Matt. "We thought we were being pretty clever about it and did our best to keep them under cover while we tried to work out a solution. But, the bad guys were pros and somehow or other we screwed up. They found out where the two were in short order. Once they knew the location, they didn't just try to take them, they tried to *kill* all four of us—the illegals *and* Lindy and me. We really thought we were done for. It was that close. They were taking us off-shore in my boat when the gal's husband and I got lucky and managed to over-take the two hoods. We were on the Intracoastal at that point. There was no question they were heading off-shore with the intention of deep sixing us. That body you saw being eaten by sharks, and the remains of that shirt, is what is left of the local Mexican Mafia's head honcho, one Miguel Delgado. Believe me, gentlemen, he was a real piece of work and a first class bastard. The other guy, Ché, was a hit man Delgado brought in to help take us out. We found his body, but we were never entirely certain if Delgado had drowned, or what had happened to him. That is, until today. Thank you, thank you, and again, thank you gentlemen!" declared Matt, raising his beer can.

"Well, you're certainly welcome. It was pure chance, of course, running across it like we did. But what an incredible story—sounds like the makings for one hell of a book," said Mike, shaking his head and reaching for another beer.

"Ya know, that's not a bad idea Captain, ah, Mike . . . funny you should mention it, I've actually thought about writing one."

"Listen," said Mike, "tell us—"

Before he could finish, Mike's cell phone rang. Listening intently to the caller, a disturbed look crept over his face. "Hon, damn it, you should have thrown the scum-ball outta' the house! I'll be right there."

Snapping the phone shut, he looked at Willy and Matt. "Sorry fellas, something's come up and I gotta run. Matt, I want to hear more about this Mexican Mafia stuff. Let's get together again, soon, over a beer."

"Terrific," replied Matt, reaching for his wallet and removing a card. "Give me a call anytime you guys are free. I look forward to it and I know Lindy would enjoy meeting you both."

"Thanks. Willy, go back out with Matt and fix him up with some jumbos. That'll get him off the hook. When we get together to learn the rest of the story, Matt here can spring for the beer."

"No way I can pass that deal up," said Matt, delighted with the arrangement.

"Come on," said Willy, looking at Matt. "I'll take ya back to Dolly; she'll fix ya up with some jumbos. I kinda think she took a liken to ya."

"Really? I'm flattered, but I'm a happily married man, Willy."

"I know, and she's a happily married gal and you're 'The Cocktail Hour Couple' and all that good stuff, but we don't have to say nothin' more about that 'til after we fix ya up with those jumbos."

CHAPTER 4

Captain Mike left the fish house and hurried along the dirt road that followed the course of the river. Between the road and the river was a mixture of small single-family dwellings, most built in the fifties and sixties. There were some one-story and a few larger, two-stories. A few had shrimp boats docked alongside their river-front homes. The area was heavily wooded, consisting mostly of pines, but there were some hardwoods and a number of large dogwoods. Several of the property owners had cleared their back yards, which sloped toward the river, and had established attractive lawns with flower and vegetable gardens.

It was a short walk to his property. Had he not been in a hurry, Mike would have remained at the fish house until all the shrimp had been removed from the holding bins and then maneuvered *Naughty* back to his own dock, as was his normal routine.

The bastard came when he knew I wouldn't be there, steamed Mike, now walking at an accelerated clip, arms pumping. As he approached the dirt road he and his dad had cleared years ago that lead through the woods to his house, five dogs of mysterious pedigrees and assorted sizes and shapes emerged from the woods and charged down the road to greet him.

Even in anger, he couldn't help but smile at this warm

reception from his canine buddies. He and Pam had acquired the dogs over time, each with its own story, and each pooch would most certainly have faced a dubious fate had Pam and Mike not intervened.

The dogs yelped and jumped, their tails wagging in delight, as they followed Mike along the dirt driveway though the woods and then settled in their usual spots on the front porch after Mike entered the house.

The house, as well as *Naughty Nina,* had been built by Mike and his dad. It sat in a cleared area, deep in the woods. It was bounded by the river along the back with two small coves of the river on either side. Due to the thickness of the woods, the neighbors could not be seen, even when the trees were barren in the dead of winter. Except for the many varieties of birds, which Mike and Pam fed and enjoyed watching, a large population of deer, which they didn't feed, and other assorted critters such as raccoons, opossums, skunks and squirrels, Mike and Pam enjoyed total privacy. It was, unquestionably, one of the choicest, most gorgeous and most desirable pieces of property in all of Varnamtown.

"Hey, I'm home," Mike announced, hanging his dark blue, Portuguese fishing cap on a kitchen chair.

Pam entered the kitchen wearing jeans and a Carolina blue *She Who Must Be Obeyed* sweatshirt. Now in her early fifties with striking, shoulder length, natural red hair, a multitude of freckles and a nice figure maintained by jogging three miles a day, practicing yoga, along with aerobics work outs on a regular basis; she was just as beautiful to Mike as the day they were married.

She and Mike had known each other since grade school and they, like most couples, had many joyful, and a few not so joyful, experiences over their years together. But with the entrance of Billy Bodean into their lives, there was no way they could have anticipated the life changing experiences they were about to encounter.

"Hi Hon, good trip, I hope?" she asked, walking over to Mike and giving him a hug and a peck on the cheek.

"Yeah, well, it was actually terrific 'til you called."

"Sorry Hon, but really, he wasn't *that* bad. He can actually be pretty nice at times. You want something, maybe a beer?"

"Yah, a beer would be fine."

Mike couldn't help notice Pam's difficulty in restraining her excitement as she lifted a *Bud Light* out of the refrigerator.

"Do I need something stronger?" Mike asked, as she handed him the Bud.

"I don't think so, well, actually, that may not be such a bad idea," she said, trying to suppress a smile.

"Then I think I'll have a rum and Diet Pepsi," he said, handing her back the beer. He was upset with Billy Bodean Dudley for having been in his home while he was away, but his anger was tempered by curiosity. Pam certainly didn't seem to be at all disturbed; quite the contrary, she was giddy with excitement.

Pam fixed the rum and Pepsi and handed it to Mike, who, not saying a word, headed out to the porch to join the dogs. Pam followed, carrying a glass of Cabernet Sauvignon for herself.

"Okay, let's have it," he said, settling into a rocker. "But before you say anything, do not, and I'm serious as I can be Pam, don't ever let that S.O.B. back in this house again unless I'm here, you got that?"

"Sure, Hon," she said, losing it, now totally unable to conceal a smile.

"Pam!"

"Okay, okay, it's just that you're not going to believe it!"

Mike knew exactly what was coming. "He raised the offer," he said. It was a statement. Mike had been expecting this, but not quite so soon. It hadn't been that long since the last offer. He took a large sip of his drink, looked out at the woods, then back at Pam. "Okay, I'm ready, let's hear it."

"A million and a half!" Pam exclaimed, leaping out of the rocker and in the process, spilling wine on her sweatshirt.

Mike's jaw dropped. An incredulous look swept his face. "What! He's offering a million and a half bucks for this place?"

"Can you believe it! That's double the last offer!"

"Jesus, I had no idea he'd go that high," Mike said, shaking his head.

He sat back in the rocker and took another large slug of the rum and Pepsi. He paused, raised the glass, drained it, stared back into it and nervously swirled the ice cubes around.

Pam sat back down, apprehensively, trying to read Mike's face for some kind of clue.

She looked down at the wine stains on her sweatshirt. "No problem," she muttered. "I can buy a bunch of them now!"

"Two things," Mike finally said, leaning forward, continuing to swirl the ice cubes.

"First is, I don't believe the bastard. You know his reputation—he can't be trusted any farther than you can throw Kong there," he said, pointing with his glass to the largest of the dogs. He lifted his glass to his mouth only to realize it was empty. "There's a catch somewhere, you can bet on it."

"Why? He'd have to come up with the money or we wouldn't sell, right?" Pam said, shrugging her shoulders in bewilderment.

"And the second thing is," Mike said, ignoring Pam's comment, "even if it's true, which I'm sure it isn't, we're not selling. We're not leaving this place."

Pam sprang from her rocker for the second time. "Mike! I can't believe you just said that! *A million and a half dollars!* That's more money than we've ever dreamed of! For God's sake Mike, we'd be rich, we'd be *stinkin', filthy rich!*"

Mike stared at Pam, wide-eyed for a few seconds, taken back by her intense reaction.

He got up from the chair and headed back into the house. "I'm bringin' out a bag of chips, a couple of Pepsis and the bottle of Bacardi—we're in for a long night."

CHAPTER 5

"Oh my gosh Matt, look at these, they're huge!"

"I know, jumbos, about twenty-five or so to the pound," Matt said, flaunting his newly acquired knowledge.

"They're every bit as big as those prawns we had in Sydney Harbor," Lindy said, "remember?"

"Are you kidding? I'll never forget it—we finished up that lunch along the water with some delectable vanilla ice cream smothered in luscious, fresh mango slices— I'd fly back tomorrow just for that!"

"You got these off the *Naughty Nina*?"

"Yup."

Matt watched as Lindy stood at the sink removing the shells, deveining the shrimp and then rinsing each one under cold water. After she finished with a shrimp, she'd drop it in a bowl of ice water. They had learned years ago to keep the shrimp chilled throughout the entire process until they were ready for cooking.

"How much were they?"

"Would you believe, *nada*? Nothing—they didn't charge me a dime."

"My goodness, you're kidding, how's that?" she said, looking up again.

"Well, to be honest, it gets pretty personal Hon, so it's probably best you don't push it."

"Oh, please, tell me, tell me."

"Okay, but remember, it's only because you insisted, and you have to promise not to get upset."

"You got it."

"Okay, well, here's the deal: I had to promise my body to Dolly."

Lindy glanced up again from the sink, "Dolly?" she asked, arching her eyebrows.

"One of the headers," Matt said.

"One of the headers?" her eyebrows remained arched.

"Yeah, one of the ladies who pops the heads off the shrimp."

Lindy paused in her task and gave Matt a look. "And you had to promise your body to her. Now I *know* I should've gone with you," she said.

"Well, yeah, but on the other hand, if you had, we probably would've gotten *much* smaller shrimp, probably medium count, about forty per pound instead of the twenty or twenty-five per pound that I got."

Lindy paused again. "I'm really afraid to ask how you know this stuff, but you're telling me these big guys are the result of your irrepressible sexuality with the shrimp headers of Varnamtown?"

"Well, modesty prevents me from taking this any further, but let's face it Hon, I've got this gift that . . ."

"Matt."

"Yah?"

"Stifle it."

"Okay," Matt laughed "but really, you should have been there."

"Why's that?"

"Where are Roberto and Maria? They need to hear this."

"Out on the beach."

"You think that's okay? Carlos is recovering pretty quickly, but still . . ."

"He's fine. The doc told him the gun wounds were almost completely healed and he could resume normal activity. Now, what's up?"

"Well, we've got a lot more in common with the *Naughty Nina* than just waving to them. Hon, *you're* not going to believe what I'm about to tell you."

"Oh good grief Matt, quit teasing and get on with it!"

"Okay, okay," Matt laughed.

He filled Lindy in on having seen their pal Curt at the dock, the story Captain Mike told of the shark attack, the shirt, and what had to be the final chapter to Matt, Lindy, Carlos and Maria's horrific encounter with Miguel Delgado and his hit man, Ché.

Wrapping up the story, Matt said, "It's pretty amazing that *Naughty Nina's* captain, the captain of the boat we see go by here all the time, and his mate, just happened to be the ones who witnessed Delgado meet his end, devoured by sharks no less. How fitting is *that!*"

"It's a huge relief finally knowing it's behind us," said Lindy, "and hopefully this will end it for Maria. She's still having nightmares about Delgado's being alive and hunting them down."

"I know. We'll fill them in when they get back," said Matt. "Listen, that's a mess of shrimp in the sink . . . let's ask Bunny and Tommy Lee over for dinner. I'll throw some Frogmore Stew together. It's simple and with these guys," he said, picking up a large shrimp, "it should be outstanding—and we'll ask Maria and Carlos to join us. Today's news is cause for celebration!"

"Good idea Hon, but before anything else, tell me this, do you know *why* it's called Frogmore Stew when there aren't any frogs in it—and if there were, *yuk*, I wouldn't eat the stuff!" Lindy exclaimed.

"I'm not sure, but I think there's a town in South Carolina called Frogmore, and that the stew is an old Gullah recipe from that area. But tell you what, I'll Google it. I'd like to know for sure myself."

"Google—whatever would you ever do without Google?"

"Most likely wallow in ignorance the rest of my life."

"Well listen, before you go Googling, *wallow* yourself over to Food Lion and get some kielbasa and small red potatoes, and then run over to Ludlum's and get some corn."

"Yes, Ma'am."

"And if you plan on using crabs this time, I think they're still some out in the traps off the dock."

"Yes, Ma'am. But I don't think so. The shrimp will be the stars of this show."

"Can you think of anything else?" Lindy asked.

"No, Ma'am."

"Matt?"

"Yes?"

"Go!"

"Yes, Ma'am."

༺✦༻

Tommy Lee and Bunny, Matt and Lindy's next door neighbors, arrived at the appointed hour. Matt and Tommy Lee sat on the front porch overlooking the Intracoastal Waterway so Matt could enjoy a Cohiba cigar along with his drink. Tonight, his drink of choice was a *Bombay Sapphire Martini*.

"Haven't had one of these in a while," Matt said, taking a sip. "Oh my," he exclaimed with a huge smile, "now I remember, 'tis indeed the nectar of the Gods."

"Wish you wouldn't sound so damn euphoric, I'm trying to swear off gin altogether," said Tommy Lee looking with some displeasure at the wine glass he was holding. "I think I'm finally beginning to acknowledge gin does funny things to my head, sorta like the same effect Valium has on me. I can handle one, but the problem is, one's never enough."

"Well, two's my limit, otherwise it's like you said, I wind up places I've never been, and to which I never want to return. A guy I worked with in Indianapolis had a real love affair with martinis. At the annual office Christmas party, after only two of them, he'd get this shitty grin on his face, lean back against the wall, sip his martini and stare at people. He'd do it all night long. He'd never say a word, just leaned against the wall and sipped and stared. You could tell by the goofy expression on his face that visions of sugar plum fairies were dancing in his head."

"Well, thankfully, I've never had that happen! Speaking of booze, I ran across a W.C. Field's quote the other day that I'd never heard."

"Which one's that? I just saw one of his old movies on Turner the other day. He was one funny man."

"Absolutely. Anyway, it went something like this," said T. L., clearing his throat and shifting into the best mode of imitating Fields he could muster. 'Reminds me of my safari trip in Africa. Someone forgot the cork screw and we had to survive for several days on nothing but food and water.'"

"I hadn't heard that one either," Matt laughed.

"Well, there's enough of 'em. Did you say Carlos and Maria are joining us?"

"Yeah, they probably need to celebrate more than we do, and we want them to start interacting more with other people. Since the Delgado thing started, Lindy and I are about the only people they've seen."

"Ya know Matt, she was really lucky not to have lost the baby that night."

"We know."

"So, where do you stand in getting them green cards, or

whatever it is that needs to be done?"

"I don't know. It's so damn complicated. The government has no idea in hell what to do about the illegal immigrants. In Carlos and Maria's case, they've applied for their green cards. Once they get them, they can apply for work permits and residency. Lindy and I are their sponsors, which basically means we're assuring the government that Carlos and Maria will not become a burden to the U.S. After that, who knows? It's a long and confusing process. They might have to return to Mexico for a while, and they're really afraid of having to do that."

Just then, Lindy popped her head out the door. "Matt, we're ready for you to put the shrimp in the pot. Everything else is done."

"Be right there. Well, half a cigar is better than no cigar," Matt said, flipping the remainder over the rail and onto the gravel drive.

"Don't give me that look T.L., they're biodegradable, and if I don't forget, I'll pick it up tomorrow morning and toss it in the trash."

"Disgusting habit, simply disgusting my friend," said T.L., slipping once again into his best W. C. Field's voice.

CHAPTER 6

"This is one of the neat parts about this dish," said Matt, as he covered the dining room table with newspapers. "Tonight, we dine as pagans."

Everyone except Lindy had a quizzical look on their face.

He returned to the kitchen and brought out a large yellow platter piled high with shrimp, kielbasa chunks, corn on the cob and small new potatoes. Steam rose from the platter as he placed it in the middle of the table.

"Frogmore Stew, ladies and gents. Just ladle the goodies onto your paper plate, peel your shrimp and toss the shells onto the newspaper along with the corn cobs. From this point on, it's hands only."

Everyone beamed smiles of anticipation.

"That looks perfectly divine," said Bunny, "we should take a picture of it!"

"Next time," Matt replied, "let's eat!"

"Matt, honey," Bunny said, "before we get started, you *promise* me there's not one single frog in there?"

"I swear Bunny, not a one."

"Well then, however in the world did it get its name?" she drawled.

"I believe we're about to hear the results of a recent Google attack," said Lindy, blinking wide-eyed at Matt.

"I'm *so* glad you asked, and it's a *search*, not an *attack*," Matt said, scrunching his nose at Lindy.

"Most people who are familiar with the dish say it originated in the small town, or what was actually the hamlet, of Frogmore, South Carolina. It's located on St. Helena Island just outside of Beaufort. However, it's my understanding the Postal Service, in its infinite wisdom, and much to the consternation of the locals, eliminated the name *Frogmore.* That's why a lot of people, not knowing the history, refer to this dish as Low Country Boil instead."

"My, *I'm* impressed," said Lindy.

"Well who actually invented it?" asked Bunny, while putting some of everything on her plate.

"It's complicated. There's some disagreement on that. Some folks think it's an old Gullah recipe, some say the local fishermen invented it, but then there's a group that gives credit to a guy named Richard Gay who was from Frogmore, owned a seafood market, and who claims to have invented the dish back in the 1980s."

By this time everyone had tasted some of everything and the murmured sounds of satisfaction rippled around the table. The pile of shrimp shells and corn cobs was quickly taking on significance.

"Okay y'all," said Bunny. "I just guess everyone except Carlos, Maria and me know what a Gullah is, right?"

Tommy Lee shrugged his shoulders and gave Matt a quizzical look.

"I don't get it," said Matt. "Why is it that I'm the only true, dyed-in-the-wool, one hundred percent, authentic damn Yankee sitting here, but I have to explain everything Southern to you red necks?"

"Matt, fess up, you knew nothing about Gullah until we stumbled across that Gullah festival down in Beaufort a few of years ago. We were on our way to Savannah with some Charlotte friends," said Lindy, dipping the ladle into the bowl and removing more shrimp. "Matt, you outdid yourself, this really is delicious."

"Thanks Hon. Okay, first let me grab another beer, then we'll have a brief course in Gullah 101. Anyone else? Carlos . . . Maria . . . *cerveza?*"

Carlos smiled and nodded affirmatively; Tommy Lee said "*Si, senor,*" and the women each shook their heads.

"Listen up, kiddies," said Matt, returning from the kitchen and passing bottles of Corona out to the men, "here's basic Gullah 101, but no questions allowed, okay?"

Everyone shook their head in agreement, although Lindy crossed her eyes, arched her neck sideways, stuck out her tongue and made a face.

"Gullahs, dear students, are those descendants of African slaves who now live in the low country of South Carolina and Georgia, including the Sea Islands, just off the coasts of both states. Some of them, mostly in Georgia, are also called *Geechees.* What they're known for is preserving, or maintaining, more of the African language and culture than any other group in this country. A lot of the Gullah language, which is beautiful to hear, but tough to understand, the food, the crafts and the music go back to their original African culture. Lindy's right, we did briefly experience the Gullah culture when we stumbled across the annual festival in Beaufort, and we enjoyed it. Okay folks, that's it, end of lesson. You'll each receive a diploma in the mail. Now, please pass the yummy platter down this way. I see several shrimp and a slice of kielbasa that have my name on them."

"When you were looking all this stuff up, did they give you some recipes like this one?" Bunny said, pointing to her plate.

"Yes, there were several. But when it comes to Frogmore Stew, I really couldn't pin down the origins."

"Well, I think it sounds much more romantic to say that the

Gullahs invented it," said Bunny.

"And I think you're absolutely right, Bunny! It's settled, a Gullah dish it is. But I have to admit that I messed with it a bit . . . a little more of this and a little less of that."

"You always do when you cook," said Lindy.

"That's half the fun, Hon."

"Hey Matt, Carlos here is a painter right?" said T. L., abruptly changing the subject.

"Right."

"Well listen, Bunny and I have been talking about how our place needs painting, the outside that is. Maybe we could hire Carlos."

"That'd be terrific Tommy Lee, I'm sure he'd love to do it. What the heck, why don't you ask him now?"

Tommy Lee looked around the table, then directly at Carlos. After taking a large sip of beer, he said, "Carlos ... I, *Yo,* ah, ... Carlos, I, ah, want-o you-o ... to paint-o mio *cassito.*"

Silence surrounded the table, followed by an outburst of laughter. Even Bunny, who knew little Spanish, realized that Tommy Lee had totally butchered his request. Lindy couldn't contain herself, tears ran down her cheeks.

"Tommy Lee," she said, regaining her composure, "I better help you out with this or Carlos will wind up painting your boat or your truck!"

Lindy turned to Carlos, and told him what Tommy Lee had in mind.

Carlos smiled enthusiastically, nodding in agreement.

"Tommy Lee, this is quite nice of you. Carlos has the time, could sure use the money, and I'm certain he'll do you a terrific job," said Matt. "Of course you'll pay him the going rate, right?"

"Well, I really hadn't thought much about that, but I'll work it out with Carlos."

Matt was certain Tommy Lee had given it considerable thought.

"I don't know, maybe I should act as Carlos's agent," laughed Matt.

"Okay, whatever," said Tommy Lee, "just remember to be fair to your favorite redneck. And now dear people," Tommy Lee continued, clearing his throat, "it's time to get down to some serious stuff. Matt, that Frogmore Stew of yours was terrific, just terrific, but when I got a beer out of the fridge earlier this evening, I hope what I saw in there was tonight's dessert."

"You scoundrel," laughed Lindy. "Yes, Tommy Lee, it is. This is indeed your lucky day, or evening. I made it with you in mind."

"Or maybe even your lucky night, if you stay on your good behavior," said Bunny softly, blushing.

ॐ

Lindy was in bed, with the small black and white Lhasa Apso pup they had just acquired, Satcha, so named after Matt's life long appreciation of Louis "Satchmo" Armstrong, nestled in the crook of her arm.

"You know," he said, climbing in, "if you were the commonest-looking lady on this island, which I hasten to add, you are not, or if you had the personality of a crab, which, again, could not be further from the truth, I swear to you that Tommy Lee would marry you just for that Cuban flan you make. I've never seen anything like it. Three damn helpings! I was hoping there would at least be a little left over for tomorrow!"

"Well, it's flattering that's for sure. And it was certainly nice of him to offer the paint job to Carlos."

"It was. I know he likes Carlos and I'm sure he'll be fair with him. I just had to razz him a little, had to give my neighbor a little grief. It was a good evening Hon, thanks."

"Thank *you*. The meal was wonderful and you certainly

sounded like the college professor this evening with all that stuff about Frogmore Stew and the Gullahs. It was fun, but now I'm ready to crash. She leaned over to Matt and gave him a peck. "Good night, Professor," she said.

Lindy turned over and quickly fell asleep. Satcha had snuggled against her neck, breathing softly—the little pup already dead to the world.

Matt was not so fortunate. He tossed and turned. It was one of those nights when nothing in particular was bothering him, but stuff just kept racing through his mind for no apparent reason.

The sound of sirens came from the direction of Ocean Blvd. The amount of anxiety when hearing sirens strangely depended upon the time of year. If it happened during the tourist season, there was, selfishly, little cause for personal concern as it happened with some frequency. With well over 10,000 fun-and-sun seeking souls on the island, chances were good that the sirens were somehow the result of a vacationer's over imbibing, or a charcoal grill that had been lit under a porch setting a house on fire, or kids out in a kayak at night just off-shore in rough water with the craft bellying up, or a grandma or grandpa, here for a family reunion, having misjudged the unfamiliar inside or outside steps of the rental house and falling. But at this time of year, with only 600 or so permanent residents, the odds of such occurrences were greatly reduced, and the possibility that the sirens being for someone they knew, significantly increased.

Matt listened as the sirens faded into the night. Hopefully, it was nothing serious for anyone, be it visitor or acquaintance. He turned, looked over at Satcha nestled up against Lindy, smiled at his two "girls," placed an arm over Lindy's shoulder, and dozed off.

CHAPTER 7

Billy Bodean paced the floor of his small office. He needed to muster some courage prior to placing the much dreaded call to Chicago. D'Agostino was going to be pissed, really pissed, no two ways about it. Billy Bodean was beginning to regret having become involved with Giacomo "The Jock" D'Agostino. But there was a bundle of money to be made. If he could pull this deal off, it would be the largest transaction he'd ever handled, and he personally stood to make a ton. Even so, as he flipped open his cell phone, his fingers shook, making it difficult to touch the appropriate numbers.

It was through a chance meeting in Litchfield, South Carolina, that this opportunity had come about in the first place. He'd been seated at the bar of a popular Litchfield watering hole, waiting for a prospective client to show. While nursing a Bud Lite he couldn't help but overhear the conversation between a couple of guys at a nearby table. Both were casually dressed, and from what he could gather of their chat, were discussing the possibility of investing, what certainly sounded to Billy Bodean, like a considerable amount of money in the area.

That was all Billy Bodean needed to hear. Far from being timid, Billy Bodean slid off the bar stool, walked over to the nearby table and introduced himself.

At first the two strangers were put off by the intrusion of this apparent local yokel, but Billy Bodean, as usual, smoothly talked his way into an invite by offering to buy the two strangers a drink.

He quickly learned they were from Chicago, and were in Litchfield for some kind of conference. They were, without question, what Billy Bodean could only describe as real Mafia looking types, and definitely Yankees, as in the *damn* variety.

Neither had gotten up, or offered his name or hand when Billy Bodean introduced himself. One of the two was heavy set with a dark complexion, black hair, graying at the temples, and black penetrating eyes. He wore a black silk, sport shirt with the top three buttons unbuttoned exposing a hairy chest, and a large gold coin held by a heavy, gold chain. The other fellow was thin with a shaved head and rimless glasses. He wore an open, light blue oxford shirt, khakis, and no jewelry.

"Billy Bodean Dudley, huh?" said black shirt. "Well Billy *Bodean* Dudley, before we get into any kind of real conversation, can you tell me why all you people down here got two fuckin' first names? It's Billy *Bodean* this and Sally *Jo* that and Betty *Jane* whatever—I don't get it."

Billy Bodean didn't get it either, but laughed. "Beats me. Guess our parents couldn't make up their minds on which names they wanted to call us, so they gave us two."

"Hey, that's good, I like that," said black shirt, looking at his companion. "You like that Allen?"

"Good a reason as any," replied Allen.

"Allen's a fuckin' thinker, not a talker, Billy *Bodean*. Sorta unusual for a mouthpiece, don't ya think?"

"Well, yeah, I guess so," said Billy Bodean.

"So what is it you do down here for a living Billy *Bodean*?" asked black shirt.

"I'm in real-estate, got my own little company, and just being up front, that's why I barged in on you fellas. I wasn't

44

being nosey, but couldn't help but overhear that you might be looking for some land. I sorta got a radar for that kind of talk."

"Oh?" said black shirt. "You got some land around here you wanna dump?"

"Well sir, I don't know if 'dump' is exactly the right word, and it's across the border in North Carolina, not here in South Carolina."

"How much you got?" asked black shirt.

"Well sir, quite a bit."

"Now Billy *Bodean*, let's understand each other right up front, I don't like to screw around . . . *quite a bit* doesn't tell me shit. So let's start with this, you got enough for a golf course?"

"Oh yes, and then some. Yes sir, sure do."

His answer grabbed the attention of both Allen and …

"I'm sorry," Billy Bodean said, looking at black shirt, "but I didn't catch your name."

"That's 'cause I didn't fuckin' throw it out, but you can just call me Jock, no no, wait, hang on here a minute, I got it, you can call me *Jimmy Joe* Jock, how's that?" he laughed. "Now I feel like I fuckin' fit right in. Jimmy Joe Jock. Hey, I like it!"

"It does have a certain ring to it," Allen laughed.

"Jock?" asked Billy Bodean, "so I guess you must have been some kind of athlete? Football would be my guess."

Both Jock and Allen choked on their drinks.

"Yeah, and I also broke the fuckin' high hurdles Olympic record," roared Jock, unable to contain himself and spraying the table with scotch and water. "Oh shit, you got a real sense of humor there Billy Bodean. I can't stand it, I gotta hit the can before I bust open."

Jock got up from the table, doubled over with laughter.

"It's been a while since I've seen him laugh like that," said Allen, watching Jock head towards the men's room, still wiping tears from his eyes. "By the way, my name is Allen, Allen Skubic." He extended his hand to Billy Bodean.

"Nice to meet you Allen, but really I don't get what's so funny," Billy Bodean said. "With a name like Jock, it seems to make perfect sense that he'd been a ball player or something."

"Nah, Billy Bodean, not even close. Jock's old man was a tough guy, a *very* tough guy in a very, ah, hazardous business, but he had one weakness: opera. He was nuts about Italian opera. When Jock was born, the old man, in a moment of extreme weakness that he forever regretted, named his son after Giacomo Puccini, the opera composer. The first name isn't spelled j-o-c-k, but it's pronounced that way. G-i-a-c-o-m-o, you know, the guy who wrote *Madam Butterfly* and *Tosca,* along with some other good stuff. The old man realized his son couldn't go through life with that moniker, so before he could even walk, they were calling him 'Jock.'"

Billy Bodean, who had not heard one note of opera in his life, and had no idea in hell what a *moniker* was, gave a knowing nod.

That same afternoon, after a couple more drinks on Billy Bodean's tab, Billy Bodean drove Giacomo *Jock* D'Agostino and Allen Skubic in his red Escalade to the area in North Carolina that he felt was perfect for their interests. Naturally enough, it was the property he owned along the Lockwood Folly River in Varnamtown.

❧

Since that chance meeting in Litchfield, D'Agostino's mood had swung one hundred and eighty degrees, resulting in Billy Bodean's extreme apprehension over placing the call to Chicago.

The deal wasn't working out as smoothly as Billy Bodean had anticipated, and the delay was infuriating D'Agostino. The track of land Billy Bodean owned along the river in Varnamtown was indeed large enough, and perfect for the exclusive, high-end country club development that D'Agostino planned to build. That wasn't the problem. The problem was that D'Agostino wanted more, specifically the house and acreage along the river owned by the shrimper, Mike Conrad and his wife. Billy Bodean had known Mike for years and had frequently bought shrimp from him. But after two substantial offers, and every bit of salesmanship, otherwise known as 'bull shit,' that Billy Bodean could muster, the Conrads continued to hold out.

Billy Bodean, with Jock's approval, offered Mike, what to Billy Bodean, was an outrageous sum for the property—a million and a half dollars. That amount would dramatically increase Billy Bodean's eagerly anticipated commission, but even then the damn shrimper still wouldn't sell. Without that location, which was adjacent to Billy Bodean's property, and precisely where D'Agostino wanted to place the club house, it was a no go. And Billy Bodean knew that D'Agostino was not the type of guy who was used to hearing the word, "No."

After several attempts, Billy Bodean's trembling index finger finally zeroed in on each of the correct numbers. Nervously listening to a couple of rings and a short pause, Billy Bodean heard, "Yeah?"

Hoping to get the conversation started off on a civil note, Billy Bodean opened with a cheery, "Hey Jock, Billy Bodean, how ya doin'? How's the weather up there?"

"Listen, that's not the fucking question numb nuts, the fucking question is, do we have the fucking property yet or not?"

"No, ah, no sir Jock, we don't ah, have the, ah, fucking property yet."

CHAPTER 8

Jock and Allen were headed north along Lakeshore Drive in D'Agostino's black Lincoln Town Car, making the short run up to Evanston. Chicago's skyline was off to their left and Lake Michigan to their right. It was a gray, cold, blustery day, with the wind blowing strong enough to form white caps on the great lake. Over the years this had become a Friday ritual, the drive north for a trout almondine lunch at *le Reve*, a superior French restaurant owned by the D'Agostino family. The restaurant being one of their few legitimate businesses.

"On crappy days like this it'd be great to just jump in the jet and head south," said D'Agostino, gazing out at the choppy water.

"Terrific idea Jock," said Allen, keeping his eyes on the busy drive. He'd much rather be in his Z4 taking the soft turns along the lake, but D'Agostino always insisted they use his Town Car, perhaps because it was bullet proof.

"All my ideas are terrific," laughed D'Agostino. "No, seriously, we put this thing together it'll be a ball buster. No one's given you any static yet, right?"

"Right, no one. A couple of the southern boys were a bit uptight about you owning a place in their territory, but they understood the convenience of having a private gathering spot more or less in the middle of the territories. God, what a great cover! By mixing in with some regular, upstanding type citizens no one will be the wiser. Did I tell you I've already contacted an architect for my southern hacienda? I can build a place down there for about a mil. The same damn place up here would run four mil, or more. Amazing."

"Let me see the plans before you get started. I don't want you screwing up the neighborhood right from the get-go," laughed D'Agostino. His spirits were good now that things were coming together for his North Carolina development. He was actually looking forward to having a southern get-a-way, while at the same time putting together an operational base for the organization.

As they were nearing Evanston, D'Agostino's cell phone rang. He opened it, took a look to see who was calling and said "Yeah?" He listened for a few moments then said, "Listen, that's not the fucking question numb nuts, the fucking question is, do we have the fucking property yet or not?"

He listened briefly, became agitated, then snapped the phone shut without saying another word to the caller.

"Our asshole realtor can't convince the asshole shrimper to sell. He said he offered a mil and a half. We need that property Allen; it's the perfect spot for the clubhouse. I was really hoping to put this thing together nice and clean like. I don't think that's gonna happen now. This is important Allen, I want you to personally get it handled."

"I'll start making arrangements when we get back from *le Reve*, Jock."

❦

Arriving back in the city after a wonderful lunch of trout almondine, Jock was dropping Allen off at Allen's office, located in the Sears Tower, inside The Loop. Allen maintained an elegant office with an impressive view of Chicago, in what was considered the most prestigious address for any business, be it local or international, in the heart of Chicago's business district.

"I wonder if anyone will ever get used to calling this place the Willis Tower," said Jock, pulling up to the curb. "What a screw up. Can you imagine how many people, every fuckin' day, including the old timers, ask, 'Who in the hell is Willis?'"

"No one likes the name change," said Allen, "Willis isn't even an American company for Christ's sake, it's some outfit based in London. Locals felt good when it was owned by Sears, an American company. Remember when the Japs were involved with the Empire State building? All hell broke lose. We still have the tallest building in the America's, but the local pride is gone. Who gives a shit about Willis?"

"It's as bad, if not worse, than when Marshall Field's changed to Macy's," said Jock. "Marshall Field's for God's sake, that and The Sears Tower were what Chicago was all about! Well, you got the fuckin' Cubs and White Socks, but who really gives a crap about them except a few thousand masochists. Then there's Maxwell Street, but no one will screw around with that, there'd be a revolution! I read somewhere about some poll that showed the change to Macy's was the worst name change in business history."

"I wouldn't doubt it," said Allen, getting out of the car. "Okay Jock, I'll get to work on our little Carolina problem and give you a report shortly."

"Good, get it done quickly Allen, no screwing around."

Allen settled into his maroon leather, executive chair,

reached into his bottom desk drawer, and removed a bottle of Johnny Walker Black and a glass. Other than an occasional glass of wine with lunch, he seldom drank during the day. However, this Carolina land purchase required a little nerve settling, a little bracer to clear the mind. It was a unique situation for him. What Jock was requesting was entirely out of his normal realm of responsibility. It was out of his Chicago comfort zone; he didn't know the people involved, he didn't know the geography, and he didn't know how business was conducted in that part of the country. There were however, two things of which he was certain: First, he would need to depend upon the asshole realtor to help him work this out, and second, of more significance, was that to disappoint Jock D'Agostino was not an option.

He took a couple of slow sips of Scotch, then told his secretary to book a flight to Myrtle Beach, South Carolina or Wilmington, North Carolina, whichever had the earliest arrival time. He'd also require a Town Car with satellite radio and a G.P.S. As for a hotel room, he'd prefer a Hilton or Marriott. After she had obtained all the confirmations, he asked her to place a call to Billy Bodean Dudley.

Billy Bodean Dudley, was at that very moment, seated at *his* desk, twisting the top off a bottle of Jack Daniels. He poured a full shot, then tossed it down. It felt soothing, really soothing. Just the ticket to settle raw nerves. Billy Bodean normally didn't drink during the day, other than the occasional Bud Light with lunch. However, this land deal with those Chicago hoods wasn't going worth a damn. He was beginning to feel apprehensive, even a bit frightened.

The latest offer to the Conrads, which he had fervently prayed would fly, had fallen through. Jock, however in the hell you pronounce his last name, had hung up abruptly on him a just a short time ago. The vibes he felt coming out of Chicago to Varnamtown, North Carolina, were taking on an ominous tone.

He knocked back another shot of Jack as his phone rang.

Checking the caller, he knocked back another quickie before picking up the receiver.

"I'll be down there tomorrow to take another look around and see what we can do," Allen informed him.

"That'll be great," said Billy Bodean, lying. "I'll pick you up."

"No need, I've rented a car."

"Okay." Billy Bodean gave Allen his office address.

"Assuming everything is okay with the property, I want you to tell me what it will take to convince those people to sell it . . . we're going to get it Billy Bodean, we're going to get it one way or the other."

"Right, you bet, absolutely," said Billy Bodean.

They hung up.

One way or the other. That didn't sound good, not at all. Maybe it would be best if this whole business would just disappear. *Damn.*

He reached for the Jack.

CHAPTER 9

Matt's unease at hearing the sirens while attempting to get to sleep proved to be prophetic. As he learned from a 3:00 a.m. phone call, his pal, Police Chief Curt Everhart, had been rushed to the hospital after having experienced a minor stroke.

After five days of concern and several hospital visits, Matt was advised that the chief was out of trouble and the outlook, positive. This good news had little impact on the chief's demeanor. His normal disposition being that of a certifiable grump, noticing any improvement, under the best of circumstances, would prove difficult.

"Get me the hell outta this zoo," was the salutation Matt received upon entering the chief's room.

"Hey, and top of the morning to you too, Sunshine," replied Matt, tossing a folded copy of the weekly *Brunswick Beacon* onto the bed. "You finally made it. You're front page news in these here parts."

The chief leaned up and grabbed the paper. "Ah, damn," he moaned, opening the paper to the front page, "Now just why in the hell did they have to do that? Of all the crappy pictures!"

"They couldn't use your academy graduation photo, their files don't go back that far. Besides, that's the real you, my good man. The real you being a somewhat mature, graying, slightly overweight—but only by a tad mind you—crime buster."

"Thanks pal," replied the Chief, continuing to scowl at the *Beacon's* front page. "I'm gonna arrest whoever took this picture and sue for defamation of character."

"You'd lose for sure, and ease up, it isn't *that* bad. They tell me you're gonna live."

"Your concern, and the *Beacon's* concern touch my heart deeply, Matthew," the chief said, finally looking up from the paper. "Yah, I'm being released tomorrow. Then confined to home detention for God knows how long."

"Nothing wrong with that Curt, you've needed a vacation for some time now. When's the last time you took any time off? Take advantage of it. When you get the green light from these guys we can take the boat out and do some fishing and crabbing."

"I'll go nuts if I can't get out Matt, you know that. I'm not a sit-on-his-ass-and-watch-TV type, and I can only read so many books and listen to so much music before going stir crazy. Oh, and here's the real kick in the keister, cigars are out, not just for now . . . forever! That stash of *Cohibas* you "confiscated" from Delgado's mansion is all yours. The only piece of good news, and it's a small piece, is that I'm allowed an occasional drink. An *occasional* drink! But of course I get to determine the meaning of *occasional.* Don't even think about imbibing in that Bombay Sapphire you've got squirreled away without me."

"I promise, unless there's a dire emergency, it'll remain sequestered only to be shared by me with our island's top cop."

"Good, and I'm gonna hold you to it. Listen Matt, I could use a ride home tomorrow. One of the boys could pick me up, but, ah, I'd rather not—about mid afternoon?"

"No problem, give me a buzz when you're cleared. Now, I gotta run. Should I let the *Beacon's* photographer in on my way out?"

"The who?"

"The Beacon's—"

The pillow missed Matt's head by inches as he ducked out the doorway.

CHAPTER 10

Heading home from the hospital, Matt thought back to when he and the chief had become acquainted. Their first encounter was at a party given by mutual friends. After that, they frequently found themselves on the back deck, or front porch of a host's residence, taking a cigar break. After several such outings, and no one else joining in, it became evident they were the only two of the usual crowd who appreciated this particular nasty, but satisfying, indulgence. And, for whatever reason, after many one-on-one conversations, they'd hit it off. But even now, after several years, Matt knew little of the chief's background. He once mentioned a childless marriage and a nasty divorce, but that was about it. Recent events with the illegal immigrants and the Mexican Mafia, had solidified their friendship. Matt now considered Curt a close, if not his closest, local friend.

There were other friends, long time friends, some stretching back to college and even two or three from those now prehistoric high school days. Realistically, many of those now fell short of friendship in the absolute sense of the word. No matter how strong or deep some relationships had been at one point, the years, distance, life choices, careers, or simply differing interests had now turned many into nothing more than, for all practical purposes, acquaintances. Links that had united, for whatever reason, had become unlinked.

When, with apprehension, Matt attended a high school reunion, college homecoming, or fraternity function designed to rejuvenate the brotherhood, he never failed to feel, (after a few beers and a rehashing of the same old stories, and singing the same old songs time after time, with little to no spirit or enthusiasm) that these events were not unlike sitting through a perpetual movie rerun, with everyone, he being the sole exception, having aged considerably.

Some enduring and deep relationships remained from the old days. Some, thank God, had even strengthened over the years, but those were the exception.

Matt couldn't put his finger on exactly why he and Curt hit it off so well. There was the mutual enjoyment of a cigar, the occasional shared shaker of *Bombay Sapphire* martinis and their mutual appreciation of big band music and jazz. This all had something to do with it. But there was no figuring it out. There was something intangible about all honest friendships. The chemistry is there, or it isn't. If it is, it doesn't require an examination or explanation. It only requires that one be eternally grateful for its existence.

Matt pulled into his driveway, finished with his philosophical musings. He was looking forward to a walk on the beach, some reading and settling down somewhere around cocktail time with a little Brubeck, Bill Evans or Miles. Not a bad plan . . . not a bad plan at all.

When he and Lindy moved to paradise, Matt had attempted, off and on, to combine two of life's pleasures—walking the beach and listening to music on his portable CD player, and later, the iPod. But, it never really worked out. Scanning the water for porpoises, shrimp boats or anything else of aquatic interest, and checking out the activities of the folks on the beach, while simultaneously listening to music, distracted from both the music and the beach. Using ear plugs, he missed the sound of the surf and the gulls, the kids squealing as they ran into the water and the laughter of the vacationers who had come to Holden Beach for some much needed R&R. So, the sights and sounds of the beach won out, and the iPod remained at home as he observed nature at its finest, including the occasional perfectly-worn bikini.

CHAPTER 11

Lindy was sitting in her reading chair in the small den off the living room when Matt walked in. The den, which had been Lindy's idea when they built the house, looked out over the Intracoastal Waterway and although small, made for a cozy reading spot. She would occasionally glance out and observe whatever waterway activity was underway. Lindy, an avid reader, belonged to two book clubs and stubbornly refused to give in to the new electronic technology, preferring print copies to any kind of an electronic tablet.

Having read *The Pillars of the Earth* a few years earlier, she was now plowing her way through Follett's sequel, *World Without End.*

"This may have been a mistake," she said, looking up at Matt. "It's exactly 1,014 pages. At this rate I won't finish 'til it's time for spring cleaning!"

"It'd make a great door stop for the back door of the garage if you want to quit now," he replied.

"No, actually it's quite good, almost as good as *Pillars,* so I'm going to stick it out. The "to read" pile will just have to continue stacking up. By the way, you had a call a few minutes ago."

"Oh?"

"Yeah, that boat captain, the one from the shrimp boat, his name and number are on the kitchen counter."

Matt headed back to the kitchen, located the note, picked up the phone, and punched in the numbers.

The captain answered on the first ring.

"Mike, Matt Paskins returning your call."

"Hey Matt, thanks for calling back. When you were over here last week we talked about getting together."

"Right, I owe you and Willy a few beers," Matt replied.

"Hey, don't worry about that. But listen, Willy and I decided to hold off for a while on fixing *Naughty* up for next season, so when you have time, we'd like to get together and hear the rest of your story."

"Absolutely! And I won't forget about the beer Mike, I'm a man of my word. By the way, the shrimp you gave us were wonderful, really terrific. I mean, they tasted better than lobster, thanks again. Hey listen, hang on a second—"

He verified with Lindy that they had no afternoon plans, and arranged with Mike to meet him and Willy at the *Paradise Cafe* on the island, for a late afternoon sandwich and a couple beers.

Before he could hang up, Lindy, having heard Matt's end of the conversation, called over to him. "Hon, I'd like to join you guys," she said. "I've been craving one of their meatball sandwiches with lots of gooey mozzarella; we can just make it our dinner."

She flashed a wide, phony smile at Matt, showing lots of teeth and rapidly fluttered her eye lashes. She waited for a reply.

"Ah, well" . . . Matt hesitated.

"Whoa, you're not telling me this is a guy thing, are you, Honey Bunch?"

"Well, no, of course not, not exactly."

"Then *exactly* what is it, Sweetums?"

Matt knew when he was cornered, got back on with Mike

and the two quickly determined it would be an excellent idea to invite the ladies. Now that Lindy and Pam were on board, the evening took on the air of a social event. They arranged to meet at Matt and Lindy's for a drink, then head to *Paradise Cafe* for dinner.

"Oh, and ask Willy to join us," said Matt, "I definitely owe him for the shrimp!"

CHAPTER 12

The three men were standing at the bar at *Paradise Cafe* enjoying a beer while waiting for the arrival of the ladies. Pam had asked Lindy if the two of them could ride together in Lindy's Miata.

"Well, those two sure hit it off pretty quick," said Willy.

"That they did," said Mike, sipping his beer. "I just hope to hell Pam doesn't get any ideas while tooling around in that Miata, but I fear the worst," he said, shaking his head.

"Lindy loves that car," said Matt. "She lets me to drive it occasionally, but with great reluctance, and God forbid I should ever get a scratch on it."

"I can see why," said Willy, "it's a good lookin' set of wheels. Hey, shouldn't they be here by now?"

"I think I know what happened," said Matt. "Lindy's been wanting to get to *The Lighthouse,* it's a favorite gift shop just on the other side of the bridge. I heard her tell Pam they're having their Fall Sale, and Pam said she'd like to take a quick look. Of course the Fall Sale, as with most gift shops and women's stores, is preceded by the Sizzlin' Summer Sale and followed by the Winter Sale and then we can't overlook the ever popular Swing into Spring Sale. There's never an end to it."

"Now I *really* fear the worst," said Mike, laughing.

They finished their beers and ordered another round just as the two wives entered *Paradise,* giggling as if they'd been pals forever. They had indeed gone to *The Lighthouse,* but would not reveal to their husbands the extent of the financial damage.

The men lifted their beers off the bar and the five of them headed to the restaurant's upper level.

Seated, the two ladies each ordered a Cosmopolitan.

Matt had covered the story of their Mafia experience over drinks at the house, so the conversation now mostly centered on shrimping and beach life.

"I love your place," said Pam, looking at Matt. "I just can't imagine how wonderful it would be to actually live on the island. And wow, that view you have overlooking the waterway, it's just too much!"

Mike shot Pam a sharp glance.

"With the housing market down like it is and everything, I bet now would be a terrific time to buy," she continued.

Mike increased the intensity of his stare.

"If you have the money, it sure would be," said Matt, not realizing that Mike wanted to get off the subject. "I don't know how much things are actually down, but I think you could buy a place for twenty-five percent to a third less than it was a couple of years ago. Maybe more. I've heard of some as much as fifty percent less. I mean, we're talking hundreds of thousands of dollars."

Willy let out a "Whew!" and took a large gulp of beer, almost choking.

"I know that's a lot of money, Willy," continued Matt, "and fortunately we built our place twenty-five years ago when things were reasonable. But there's no question that the market's still way down."

Pam looked over at Mike, whose fixed stare had not left, but now, in addition, was shaking his head. After all their years together, he could read her like the proverbial book. They could live here on the beach just like Matt and Lindy and still have well over half the money left—even after the purchase of a shiny, new sports car.

"Well actually, we sorta like it where we are, don't we, Hon?" said Mike, never taking his eyes off Pam. "My family has lived in Varnamtown for three generations; I just can't imagine living anywhere else. My dad and I built the house we live in. Why on earth would we ever want to leave?"

"That's wonderful, and I can sure understand your reluctance. My family, and for that matter, Matt and I, moved around a lot. We never had the pleasure of enjoying those kind of roots," said Lindy. "I was thinking the other day, it's hard to believe, but our place at Holden Beach is our thirteenth home!"

"Well, all I can say is, thirteen must be your lucky number," said Pam, "because you sure have a great place." She was trying hard to steer the conversation back to beach living. Unfortunately for her their waitress returned to the table at that moment to take the dinner orders.

As the waitress was getting her pad and pencil in position she said, "I guess you heard about all the excitement, huh?"

The five of them looked up at her, and Willy asked, "No, what excitement's that?"

"Well, I don't know exactly for sure, but everyone down at the bar is saying there's some kind of mess, something about a big fire happening over in Varnamtown," she replied.

CHAPTER 13

They left *Paradise Cafe*, crossed the bridge, hung a right at the light and sped toward Varnamtown. Matt and Lindy, with the top down, followed the others in her Miata.

"I hope everything's okay," said Lindy, tucking her hair under her red Holden Beach cap. "I guess when anything happens in Varnamtown, it's everyone's concern."

"I think you're right," said Matt "They're a tight bunch over there."

"I really like Mike and Pam," said Lindy. "Oh, and of course Willy . . . he's a cute old guy."

"Nice folks all," said Matt, looking ahead and keeping a safe distance between the two cars.

"Pam would move to the beach in a flash if given the chance," said Lindy

"Well, who in the heck wouldn't?" replied Matt.

"There are those who prefer the mountains, ya know," said Lindy.

"Yeah, but we both also know those people are weird," Matt laughed.

"We have some very good friends who wouldn't appreciate that caustic comment in the least," replied Lindy.

They passed the Tri Beach Fire Department on Sabbath

Home Road and were now on Varnamtown Road headed straight for the docks. Matt was the first to catch a faint whiff of smoke. He looked over at Lindy, whose eyes widened as she picked up on the scent.

Moments later, slightly off to the left, low in the sky, they saw a faint orange glow.

"He's seen it," said Matt. Mike's truck had accelerated.

The closer they got to the river, the faster Mike drove. Matt was certain Mike would head straight for the docks and was surprised when he hung a left at the curve onto Ebb Tide Lane. At this point Mike was flying, his car fish tailed as he took the curve, but he pulled it out and kept going.

Matt shot Lindy a glance. "This isn't good Hon. He's really panicked."

They swung onto a dirt road which Matt was certain followed the river. Although thick with trees and brush, it was easy to see where they were headed. There was a fire, it was a big one, and it had to be along the river, not too far ahead of them.

The area remained heavily wooded with no houses in sight. They came to a small clearing, and Mike's truck skidded to a stop. There was a house sitting in the middle of the clearing, and behind the house, the sky was orange.

Mike, Pam and Willy flew out of the truck and ran toward the back of the house. Matt pulled in behind Mike's truck and he and Lindy scrambled out to follow the others.

Reaching the back, Matt and Lindy froze in place. Staring down the incline to the river, they saw Mike on his knees, his head twisting from side to side, his face grossly distorted in anguish. His clenched fists violently pounded the ground. They saw Willy, his arms wrapped around Pam, her face buried in Willy's shoulder as her body heaved in uncontrollable sobs. Just beyond them, in the water, they saw flames leaping, lighting up the night sky. A boat was ablaze in the water. Even through the smoke and intense fire, Matt and Lindy recognized the outline of a shrimp boat. They both knew that it wasn't just any shrimp boat, it was the *Naughty Nina.*

❧

They sat in silence at the kitchen table, Willy, slumped in his chair, slowly shaking his head from side to side in shocked disbelief.

Matt was thinking he and Lindy should leave. This was a personal tragedy for Pam and Mike, and Willy for that matter. They should be left alone. There was nothing that either of them could say or do to alleviate the deep pain and sense of loss these three were feeling.

Before Matt could say anything, Mike shoved his chair back, said "Ah shit," mostly to himself, got up, went to the refrigerator and returned with five bottles of beer.

"Anyone want something stronger?" he asked. "I do, but first I gotta wash that god damn taste out of my mouth and throat."

He twisted the caps off the beers, passed them around, and sat back down.

He sat with both hands on the beer bottle and spent several moments staring at it, turning it in his hands, peeling the label off. He looked up at the group of solemn faces.

"Listen," he said, "there's something I need to tell y'all. We haven't known each other very long, but I feel we've developed a pretty fast and close friendship."

"We have," Matt agreed.

Lindy nodded her head.

"Willy, I hadn't said anything to you about this yet either, 'cause I was afraid you'd worry yourself to death."

A puzzled look crossed Willy's face.

"I gotta back up for a minute. But first, ya'll have to understand something—what happened to *Naughty* tonight wasn't any damn accident. I'm certain of it. Someone set her on fire. She was torched."

Each of the others at the table could not have been more surprised.

"And the reason it was done," Mike continued, "was to scare the hell out of me and Pam, not to mention along with putting me out of business and ruining our livelihood." Mike took a long pull on his beer. "Here's the deal, and please, keep this confidential. No one else needs to know anything, not yet. Not 'til I got it all figured out. Okay?"

They each nodded, wondering where Mike was headed.

"We've been offered a ton of money for this house, well, for the entire property for that matter. Some builder wants it for some kinda highfalutin development. Big homes, mansions, fancy private golf course; all that kind of big money stuff. Billy Bodean, the realtor, and if you don't know him, I can tell you he's a real piece of work, has been bugging the hell out of us to sell—keeps jacking up his offer. If I told you where it's at now, you probably wouldn't believe me." Here Mike hesitated, took a second long pull on his beer and said, "but I'll tell you this much, it's north of a million bucks."

Willy choked on his beer for the second time that night.

Matt and Lindy weren't surprised. Although the market was down, they'd witnessed the dramatic increase in property values along the coast over the past several years. A million dollars might be on the high side, but it wasn't out of line for the right location. An upscale development, located along the water, translated to premium property. From what little they had seen, Mike's location qualified as premium.

"But I'm not gonna sell," said Mike. "Like I told you earlier, my Dad and I built this place, just like we built *Naughty,* that beautiful boat that's out there dying on the water right now.

And believe me, a part of me is out there dying right along with her." If anyone bothered to look directly at his face, they'd see that Mike's bloodshot eyes had again glossed over.

He paused, spread his arms wide and looked around. "But *this*," he said, "this is my *home* and no one is gonna take *this* away from me! We're not leaving this place. We're water people. What the hell do we need a million bucks for? We don't want it, and we don't need it! We got this! Listen, we're not bridge players, or golfers or cocktail-party types. No insult intended guys, you know what I mean. Oh, there're some here who go for that stuff, and that's okay, that's just fine, but it's not *us*. It's not me and Pam. Along the river here we're shrimpers and crabbers. We're clammers and oystermen and fishermen. That's who we are. I swear," exclaimed Mike, his voice now trembling, "if anyone tries to take this away, I swear to God I'll kill them. I'll kill whatever son-of-a-bitch even *thinks* about it!" His beer bottle nearly shattered as he slammed it onto the kitchen table.

"Mike!" Pam hollered. "Stop! You can't talk like that!"

Mike looked around the table, his face flushed, his hands shaking. Embarrassed, he took a deep breath. "I'm sorry," he said. "I guess it's time for a touch of the hard stuff to settle the nerves. Please, I know I've made it difficult for y'all, but stay for a nightcap. I'd really appreciate it."

≈

Willy and Pam walked Lindy and Matt out to their car.

"It's gonna take a long time for Mike to get over this," Pam said, "if he ever does. *Naughty* was a part of him, and every time he went out on her, he felt his dad was with him. Well, to be honest about it, *Naughty* was a part of all of us."

"It has to hurt something awful," said Lindy. "I just hope he doesn't do anything foolish."

"You can bet I'm gonna stick pretty close by," Willy said. "I've seen him madder than all get-out a few times, but I ain't ever seen him anything like this."

Inside, Mike finished his rum and Pepsi, poured another and headed out the back door. He walked down the incline to the dock and got as close to *Naughty* as he could. The firemen were gone, the helpers had left and the friends and neighbors had drifted off. *Naughty* was still smoldering in spots, but the fire was over and the damage done. He sat on the back edge of the dock, pulled his legs up under his chin and wrapped his arms around his legs. He looked up into the star-lit night. It was clear and crisp, with a nearly full fall moon reflecting brightly off the water of the Lockwood Folly River.

Sorry Pop, damn, I'm so sorry. I never thought it would come to anything like this. But I promise you Pop, I absolutely swear to you, I will get the bastards who did this to us.

Mike glanced over the charred remains of *Naughty*. He raised his head back up, again staring into the night sky, tears streaming down his face. He buried his head in his hands. His sobs of anguish and despair could be heard across the water and throughout the marshland he so dearly loved.

CHAPTER 14

At mid morning, Matt made a run across the bridge to *The Bookworm* to buy a copy of Tom Reiber's, *The Nine Irony*. He was picking the chief up at the hospital later in the day and thought Tom's book, a guy themed mystery, would make a nice convalescence gift. Reiber's a local writer and this was his first published work. A central protagonist in the story is a gruff police chief with whom Matt thought his pal Chief Curt Everhart could readily identify.

Approaching the bridge, he slipped *Satch Plays Fats* into the CD player. Matt had been enthralled by Armstrong's playing since being a teenager, had even seen him in person while still in high school . . . and had owned this particular session since it first appeared on LP in the mid-fifties. Now of course, he had the CD and had also loaded it onto his iPod. Fats Waller had written a lot of up-tempo, fun tunes like *Your Feet's Too Big, The Joint is Jumpin', Ain't Misbehavin'* and, of course, *Honeysuckle Rose*. But the real gem of this session, the pure stroke of genius, in Matt's opinion, was Armstrong's rendition of *Black and Blue*. Sung in a slow, haunting rhythm, Matt knew that way back he had heard other versions without getting the real meaning, but with Armstrong's rendition, he got it . . . it was impossible to miss.

With lyrics like:
    I'm white, inside
    But that don't help my case,
    'Cause I can't hide,
    What is in my face.
 Then this:
    How will it end,
    Ain't got a friend,
    My only sin is in my skin,
    What did I do, to be so black and blue?

Waller had never written a more poignant song and Armstrong had never sung with more emotion. Matt got chills listening to it again as he pulled into *The Bookworm's* parking lot.

Once inside, with *Black and Blue* still bouncing around in his head, he saw there were a few browsers, some of whom Matt knew. It being past the peak season, the store's business, until next spring, would consist largely of locals. It had a separate room for romance, children's books, mysteries, etc., and was the cozy kind of place the locals liked to drop by to chat and visit, particularly with Jim and Barbara, the two knowledgeable proprietors.

Normally, Barbara would have *WHQR*, the NPR station out of Wilmington on for background music. When the station switched to talk radio in the afternoons, her CD player would go to work, often sending some Chopin or Beethoven flowing through the store's various rooms.

Matt approached the counter where Mel Peck, Steve Lehr, Carol Miller and Bev Spier, each friends of Matt and Lindy's, were discussing the upcoming election. He knew how these conversations normally went, and prepared himself to avoid any involvement.

As in most small towns, politics was a blood sport and

certainly not for the faint of heart. Seldom do the locals identify themselves as Democrats, Republicans or Independents for that matter. It was more a matter of who knew who, who's father did what to who's father or mother, which family had shafted another family, who got divorced from whom, lied, drank too much, drank too little, snubbed somebody at the grocery store, or, not having been invited to a party they "shoulda been," took it as a personal insult, and the "friendship" was flat-out terminated.

It was the "good guys" vs. the "bad guys," or, as some liked to put it, "us" vs. the "dark side." Conversations could become intense regarding the war in Afghanistan or the President's plans for health care, and the discussions were often hot and heavy, but when over, the friendships endured and life went on. But get into a discussion regarding the town budget, or where, or if, to plant a couple dozen palm trees, or where to place swing set, or whether or not to build a community center, well then, tensions ran high and relationships became strained.

The hot conversations this election evolved around whether or not to build a community center on the island. One side maintained the island needed such a center as a gathering place for both residents and visitors alike. The opposition insisted the old building was still quite adequate, the town couldn't afford a new one, and "why in the hell do we need to build a place for visitors anyway when we've got the damn beach right out there and that's what in the hell they come for in the first place." The "dark side" was in favor of the center, and the "good guys," made up primarily of a more financially conservative group of retirees, was adamantly against it.

"So Matt, where are you on this community center thing?" asked Carol, as Matt approached the group.

"Oh, no, surely you jest Carol. Is that what you guys are discussing? I just popped in to pick up a few books. Pretend you didn't see me."

"Why's that?" Carol asked, "it's the most important issue

we've got on the island, and as a friend, I value your opinion."

"Come on, Carol, you're not going to suck me in. Listen, I learned years ago not to discuss politics or religion with friends, not if I care to keep 'em. There's no middle ground on this community center thing. If you get into an argument over it, I promise you, it's gonna affect the relationship. It may not be apparent, in fact it may be very subtle, but trust me, it'll change things. I've seen friendships, even close family relationships, destroyed over politics. I'm not kidding, and I sure as hell ain't gettin' involved in this conversation because I love y'all so very dearly!"

"Now that was spoken like a true diplomat, Matt. You know, it's not too late, you could still run for one of the Town Commissioner spots as a write-in," Carol said.

"Oh good grief! What's that saying, 'I may be dumb, but I ain't stupid?' Why anyone would run for *any* public office, national, state or local is beyond me. No matter what decision you make, it's going to tee some people off. I don't want to tee people off. I'm a lover, and I wanna be loved. I need affection, I need embracing! In fact, I could use a hug this very moment. Carol, come over here and give me the kind of big, warm embrace for which I desperately yearn."

"Oh good God, I take it that's a no," said Carol.

"Duh," Matt replied, smiling. "You got *that* right!"

"Hey Matt," Steve said, "Guess you heard about that shrimp boat burning down over in Varnamtown."

"Well yeah, I did. Actually, Lindy and I were there," Matt said.

"What?" said Steve. "How's that?"

"We were at *Paradise Cafe* last night for dinner with Mike Conrad and his wife. They own the boat. We were just finishing up when the waitress told us there was some kind of trouble over in Varnamtown. Since the Conrads live there, we rushed right over. When we got close, we could tell by the sky that there was a fire, and it was in the vicinity of his home. Sure enough, when we got to his place, his shrimp boat, the *Naughty Nina*, was blazing away like crazy. It was horrendous, really horrendous. Mike and his wife are devastated. I've never seen two people in such pain, not even at a funeral. By the time we left, I felt we had been to a wake."

"I know that boat," said Carol, whose home is on the Intracoastal. "It goes by our place all the time."

"Right, along the Intracoastal, going out or coming back into Varnamtown," said Matt. "When we left last night, Mike and his wife were a mess, but there wasn't anything Lindy and I could do. *Naughty* was not only their livelihood, but they considered her a member of the family. I guess in many respects, she was. Mike and his dad built her when Mike was in high school back in the 50's. She was barely floating when we left last night and has probably sunk by now. Thankfully, no one was injured. We're going over this afternoon and see if there's anything we can do for them."

"There's already a rumor floating around that arson is involved," said Bev.

"Nobody will know anything until the inspectors do their thing. Mike kinda thinks it was arson, in fact, he seems pretty certain of it."

"For God's sake, now just who in the hell would do something like that to a shrimper?" asked Steve. "Those guys are barely scraping out a living as it is, everybody knows that. Arson doesn't make any sense . . . bastards!"

Matt decided there was no need for further elaboration. He knew Mike's suspicions, at this point, were unfounded.

He walked over to the local author's rack and found Reiber's book. Barbara reached under the counter and brought out two books Matt had special ordered. He was checking out when his cell phone rang.

It was Lindy. "Yeah, Hon."

"Matt, Pam just called, she needs your help right away."

"Why, what's going on?"

"Mike just stormed out of their place. Matt, he's carrying a gun. Willy tried to stop him, but Mike shoved him aside. She's certain he's gone looking for Billy Bodean, that realtor guy, but she's afraid to get the police involved so she called here for you. She says he'll listen to you. She wants you stop him before he gets into serious trouble."

"Just how in the hell am I supposed to do that?"

With Matt hollering, and the group hearing Lindy screaming on the other end, all eyes were on Matt.

"I don't know! Don't get upset with me Matt! I'm just doing what she told me to do!"

Matt, looked around, realized he was the center of attention, and lowered his voice.

"Okay Hon, I'll try," he said.

He laid the books back on the counter, told Barbara he'd return for them later in the day, and headed out the door.

Back in his car, he figured the best place to start was to find Billy Bodean's office in Varnamtown. Chances were it was on the town's main drag. He called Lindy back and asked her to check the phone book for Billy Bodean's address. Not knowing his last name, it took a few moments before she saw the small display ad in the yellow pages for Billy Bodean's company.

While waiting for Lindy to find the address, Matt's mind flashed back to the danger he and Lindy had faced earlier: Lindy bringing the illegal Mexican couple into their home to hide them from the Mexican Mafia, the wife, Maria, being pregnant, the Mafia locating Maria and Carlos and then the near-death experience of both the illegal couple along with Lindy and himself at the hands of the two hoods on the waterway, the fight on the boat, the gun shots, the wounds. He and Lindy were supposed to be leading tranquil, enjoyable, uneventful lives in retirement. *What the hell was happening?*

Matt pulled out of *The Bookworm* parking lot and hung a left onto the same road he and Lindy had traveled the night before, a night they wouldn't soon forget. And now, because of this situation with Mike, he was racing down it once again.

Well damn, he mumbled aloud while shaking his head, *I don't believe it, here we go again.* And then, with a half smile, he couldn't help but think of Count Basie's version of *April in Paris* ending with his instructions to the band to *"Play it one more time!"* Unfortunately, he had no idea how this new situation was going to end and this could be "one more time" too many.

Back in *The Bookworm*, Mel Peck looked at the small pile of books Matt had left on the counter. On top was *The Nine Irony,* the next one down was Michael Connelly's latest, *The Drop,* and at the bottom of the pile was a new biography of Thelonious Monk.

Mel Peck looked around at the group with a quizzical expression.

"Who in the heck, or just *what* in the heck, is a Thelonious Monk?"

CHAPTER 15

Ignoring speed limits, Matt made it to Varnamtown in under five minutes. There was no need to check addresses. He spotted Mike's pickup off to the right, parked in a gravel driveway in front of a red brick, single-story, office building. A small yard sign declared simply, *Dudley Realty.* In his many trips to Varnamtown's waterfront, Matt had never noticed the sign.

With the tires tossing white gravel, he skidded into the drive, jumped out of his car and ran to the front door. Grabbing the handle he flung the door open, then froze in place.

Billy Bodean sat staring up from his desk at Mike Conrad, who stood directly in front him. Mike had one arm extended. In his hand he gripped a pistol. It was firmly pressed against Billy Bodean's forehead.

Neither man looked at, nor spoke to Matt. He took a couple of tentative steps into the office.

Billy Bodean's face was flushed, his eyes bulged, his forehead covered in sweat. Tears streamed down his cheeks.

"I didn't do it, Mike! I didn't do it! You gotta believe me! I swear to Christ I didn't do it!"

Mike shot a quick look over at Matt.

"Why are you here? How'd you find me?"

"Pam called. She knew you went out looking for this guy,"

Matt replied. "I had a hunch this would be the first place you'd try."

"He did it, Matt. This lying sack of shit did it and I'm going to blow his cruddy little brains all over his cruddy little office."

Billy Bodean tried to turn his head to look at Matt, but Mike pushed the pistol even harder against Billy Bodean's skull.

"I don't know who you are, but please talk to him," Billy Bodean begged of Matt. "I didn't touch his boat! No way I'd do something like that! Please tell him!"

"He did it, Matt. This bastard will do anything to get my property. Everybody in town knows he's a slime-ball with no scruples." Mike said. "For this kind of a sale, he'd spit on his mother's grave."

"Look, Mike," Matt said. "you're upset, you're royally pissed and I understand that. But Mike, there's no proof at this point. You don't know for absolute certain."

"The only proof I need is knowing this asshole well enough to know he did it."

"So, based on a hunch, you're willing to throw your life away by killing this *asshole*?"

Matt inched closer to the two men.

"Even if you had proof, Mike, you don't want to screw up your and Pam's life. This guy can't be worth all that."

Matt took a couple more steps and was now standing directly in front of the desk . He held out his hand.

"Give it to me, Mike, you might make a mistake and actually kill the bastard. Let me have the gun and we'll go about getting to the bottom of this, but within the law. I'll help you. But don't make a mistake now that you'll regret forever. Now I'm asking you, *please* give me the damn gun."

Mike was staring straight into Billy Bodean's terrified eyes. His hand still pressed the pistol hard against Billy Bodean's forehead. A finger remained on the trigger.

Except for Billy Bodean's whimpering, the office was quiet.

"Please," Billy Bodean cried, tears streaming down his face. "Mike, I'm begging ya, please don't do this."

There was a long, tense pause. No one spoke. No one moved. No one in the room knew what would happen next.

"Ah shit," Mike said, lowering the pistol and handing it to Matt.

CHAPTER 16

The fire had not totally destroyed *Naughty*. There was a possibility of saving her. Well, at least enough of her remained salvageable for Mike to feel he would still be shrimping on the old *Naughty*. After some agonizing soul searching and several sleepless nights, Mike decided he'd rather restore her than build or buy another boat. Prior to that decision, he seriously considered tossing in the towel. The substantial time, money and sweat required in the restoration process was a reality. The critical problems confronting the local shrimping industry were a reality. But in the end, he knew that until the industry, or possibly age, forced him to hang it up, he'd remain what his family had been forever—shrimpers. It was in his blood. It was who he was. He had to continue doing what he loved to do.

Several weeks had passed without further word from Billy Bodean. Mike and Pam assumed that after the incident in Billy Bodean's office, the realtor had given up any thought of acquiring their land. That, or after having the be-Jesus scared out of him, he was too frightened to pursue it further.

In some respects, Mike was surprised. The more he thought about what kind of development could be built, and what kind of money could be made by whoever was behind it, the more he believed that the folks with the deep pockets would make another run at him. On the other hand, if they were behind the boat burning, which he was certain they were, the pressure could come from another angle. He tried hard not to think about that, and he never mentioned this thought to Pam.

Pam realized chances didn't look good, and in fact were pretty slim, but she secretly continued to harbor the hope that another offer would be made, one that Mike simply would not be able to resist. The thought of a beach house, and a neat convertible sports car, had grown from wishful thinking to something just short of an obsession. She embraced the thought of finding out what it would like to be rich. Not that they'd ever had it that rough, but *rich* certainly had a nice ring to it.

But no matter what the outcome, the two couples realized that some good had been born out of the *Naughty Nina* tragedy. The Conrads and the Paskins had struck up a pleasant friendship over the weeks following the horrible night of the fire. The two couples had gotten together several times socially, and Lindy and Pam had become phone as well as shopping buddies.

Chances of this happening at this stage in their lives, particularly coming from such diverse backgrounds and cultures, were remote. But each realized that a unique and wonderful thing had happened. It was a relationship of no pretenses, no phoniness, no one-upmanship—just an honest, warm, fun, new found friendship for which they were thankful and in which they delighted.

Of course the speculation and theories regarding the fire were occasionally discussed, but that situation had mostly faded into the background.

That is, with the exception of Mike's well-masked pent-up anger.

CHAPTER 17

Jock and Allen were seated, having drinks in the luxury condo Jock owned along the lake in Evanston, just north of Chicago. Jock owned the entire complex and had taken the top floor of one of the several buildings for his own. Conveniently located within walking distance of *le Reve*, the condo served as Jock's sanctuary and love nest. To the best of Allen's knowledge he, along with Jock's mistress, were the only two people who knew about the place. Jock, some time ago, had told Allen it was available to him if he needed a discreet location to get laid, but Allen had never taken Jock up on the offer. There were some things, for whatever reason, Allen felt it best that Jock not be aware of, his occasional tryst being one of them.

This particular evening however, sensual pleasure was the least thing on either man's mind.

Jock got up from the couch, walked over to the large, curved, teakwood bar and stood mixing another Manhattan, his favorite drink.

"You want one?" he asked, looking over his shoulder at Allen. "I make the perfect Manhattan, ya know, two parts a good Canadian blend, none of that cheap shit, and one part Martini-Rossi sweet vermouth. Stir in a little ice, give it a nice shake, and *voila',* you've got yourself the absolute, perfect Manhattan.

Some people screw it up with bitters or drop a fucking cherry in it. La-de-dah like, ya know? It was also my old man's favorite drink. Every night when he came home from work my mom would have a pitcher of Manhattans in the fridge waiting—ya sure?"

Allen was shaking his head. "No, but thanks, I'll stick with the Cabernet. He lifted the bottle off the cocktail table and refilled his glass. "I gotta drive back into the city. Don't want to take any chances with the hard stuff."

"That's what I like about you Allen . . . very level headed . . . very steady . . . you know how to do the right thing. That's why I depend on you. On the other hand, well, listen, you've worked for me for a hell of a long time, right?"

Allen nodded his head.

"And I've always shot straight with you, never any bullshit, right? Well, not much."

Allen again nodded his head, aware now of why they were having drinks and also acutely aware, from having witnessed it with others, that he was about to receive a tongue lashing.

"Right, so I'll tell you like it is—so far, you've royally fucked up the Carolina deal. It shoulda' been in the bag by now. It shoulda been handled a long time ago. What the hell's wrong? You've never let me down like this."

"I know," said Allen, shaking his head, "and you've got every right to be pissed. I don't get it Jock, I just don't get it. We've offered at least three times what that damn property is worth, and when the money wouldn't do it, we tried some muscle with the boat and the son-of-a-bitch still won't budge."

"Not that I really give a shit, but how did you handle the fire? That ain't necessarily your area of expertise."

"It was pretty simple, the toughest part was keeping that dumb shit Dudley from blowing us up. I've got five cans fully loaded with gas on the boat, he's shaking like, what's his name, Don Knotts, and the dumb shit decides to have a cigarette! It was almost comical. I slapped the damn thing out of his mouth just as he was getting ready to light up!"

"Well, there ya go," said Jock, grinning for the first time. "That's some positive news. Now our good 'ol boy's gotta realize he's in this up to his friggin' red neck. There ain't no turnin' back for Billy Bob."

"Billy Bodean," said Allen. "Anyway, I rented a small johnboat from a nearby marina. Billy Bodean guided me up the river that night to, what the hell's it called . . . Varnamtown, or something like that, where the shrimp boat was docked. I doused the boat with the five cans of gas, set a delayed fuse, then we quietly cruised back down the river at a casual pace. By the time we noticed the orange sky, we were long gone. We docked the boat back at the marina. It was closed by then. I caught a flight out of Myrtle Beach early the next morning. It probably didn't take long for them to realize it was arson, but I didn't see any other way of pulling it off, particularly as I didn't want to involve anyone else."

"Well, the only thing I see wrong with *that* plan," said Jock, "is that it didn't fucking work."

There was no missing the sarcasm in Jock's voice.

Jock walked back to the bar to mix another drink. Allen took the opportunity to refill his glass, however, this time, as he poured the wine he noticed a tremor in his right hand. He nearly missed the glass. As tight as they had been for many years, Allen sensed the relationship was being tested. For the first time since starting to work for Jock, he experienced a tinge of personal fear. Over the years he had witnessed first hand that being the recipient of Jock's wrath was most unpleasant. It was to be avoided.

Jock finished mixing his drink and turned back to Allen. "Listen, here's the bottom line; there's no more screwing around with this, you understand? Not only do I want it, I want it *now*. My reputation is on the line here. I don't pull this off, I look like shit. It could screw up some other plans I got. Now you, Allen, get your well-educated ass back down there and deal directly with this shrimping guy. If he has any smarts, he's gotta realize by now this ain't something involving just that asshole realtor. He *knows* somethin' bigger is going down, and if he doesn't, you can make it very clear to him—nice and personal like . . . ya know what I mean?"

Of course Allen knew exactly what Jock meant, and he didn't like it worth a damn. Until this situation had come along, his relationship with, and responsibilities for Jock had been purely cerebral . . . getting and attempting to keep Jock out of trouble with the law, advising him on personal and financial issues, managing Jock's Swiss account and other off-shore accounts, and acting as Jock's overall confidant. Others were employed by the organization to perform the grunt work. This Carolina property deal had taken Allen in a direction he most certainly had not signed on for. And it was obvious this evening that it had definitely become a game changer in their relationship.

"Sure, Jock, I understand its importance to you and I know what you mean. Consider it done."

"And listen, Allen, the next time I hear from you, that's exactly what I want to hear: *it's done.* I don't care what it takes or how you do it. Take the gloves off, get tough and wrap this fucker up *now.*"

Allen drained his wine glass and left the condo, having no idea about his next step. One thing was certain; no matter what the next step, he knew it would lead him further down a path he no longer cared to travel.

Allen Skubic grinned and shook his head as he walked to his car. *Mom was right,* he thought, *I should have become a foot doctor like she wanted . . . my brother Karl . . . he listened . . . he's most likely sitting comfortably in his boat in Naples Harbor at this very moment . . .probably sipping a glass of Merlot, or pulling in a snook, while I get to do some crappy work for an egomaniac who's eventually gonna screw up my life . . . I can feel it coming . . . yup, shoulda listened to Mom.*

The next morning, after determining the first priority was to return to North Carolina, he had his secretary make new travel arrangements. By the time he hit the Carolina coast, he hoped to have a plan in place.

He flew into Myrtle Beach after changing planes in Charlotte and having been amazed at the size and activity of that city's terminal. He knew Charlotte had a so-so NFL team and a floundering NBA team, but other than that, he knew nothing, nor had heard anything about the town. So why this huge terminal with all its hustle and bustle? He'd have to check it out.

He experienced similar thoughts regarding Myrtle Beach, but had at least heard of it over the years. He picked up his car, tuned to *Seriously Sinatra* on Sirius Radio, locked in Billy Bodean Dudley's address on the GPS, and headed for Varnamtown.

He had made several attempts at reaching Billy Bodean at his office and on his cell phone, all to no avail. When he arrived at the Varnamtown office, it was closed. Allen had developed a plan of action, but it was risky and would require the assistance of the realtor. Not wanting to pursue it further until meeting with Billy Bodean, he got back in the Town Car determined to find a decent place to grab some lunch. Heading back toward Shallotte, he noticed the sign for Archibald's Deli and pulled in.

He ordered a Reuben sandwich and had to admit to himself it was every bit as good as he'd get in Chicago, if not better. On his way out, he held the door for a couple, exchanged a greeting with them, and thought he'd make a quick run back to Billy Bodean's in the event the red neck had returned. He had. It was time to get down to business. It was time to turn up the heat.

CHAPTER 18

Pam and Mike pulled into Archibald's parking lot. They were there to meet Matt and Lindy for lunch.

As they entered, the door was held open for them by a stranger who was on his way out. He head was shaved and he wore rimless glasses. Both Pam and Mike sensed he wasn't from Southeastern North Carolina.

"Thanks," said Mike, as he passed through, "and have a great day."

"Oh, I'm counting on it," the stranger replied.

Mike and Pam looked at each other, heading for a table. "Yankee," they said in unison to each other, and laughed.

They were no sooner seated than Mike looked out the window and saw Matt and Lindy pulling into the parking lot, just as the stranger pulled out in a black Lincoln Town Car.

The four had decided on Archibald's, a favorite lunch spot of the locals and vacationers. Owned and operated by Rose and Bob, it featured an excellent deli type menu with daily specials prepared by Chef Bob. Rose handled the front. With her effervescent personality, she had absolutely no compulsions about joining any table conversation that happened to perk her interest.

Chef Bob stayed pretty much behind the counter, but would also jump into the fray if so inspired.

"Ya know, when you think about it, chances of this happening are pretty slim," Mike said.

"Chances of what happening?" asked Rose as she placed four iced teas on the table.

"The chances of Lindy, originally from Cuba, meeting Matt, originally from New Jersey, and then Pam and me coming from the recognized center of the universe, Varnamtown, getting together here in southeastern North Carolina. It's pretty neat, don't you think?" Mike asked, looking at Rose.

"Yeah, it is," Rose replied. "Bob and I are from Baltimore. It's amazing how we each found our way here."

"Baltimore?" Mike asked, raising his eye brows.

"Yes, Baltimore," said Rose, "and seeing that look on your face I gotta remind you that Baltimore is *south* of the Mason-Dixon line, so don't give me that *she's a damn Yankee look.* You better warn him, boyfriend," she said, smiling at Matt. "I've been known to miss the cup when pouring a refill."

"Ouch," said Mike, laughing and placing his hands on his lap.

"In fact," said Bob, now being drawn into the conversation having overheard the chit chat from behind the counter, "some Civil War historians will tell you that the first blood of the Civil War was drawn in Baltimore. Seems local Confederate sympathizers tangled with some Massachusetts militia who were on their way to Washington. They'd been ordered there by Lincoln."

"Come on, get out of here, it started in Baltimore? I don't believe it," said Matt.

"Hey, it's true! Look it up! Google it," said Bob.

"Dear Lord, not again," said Lindy, shaking her head.

"Do y'all want to hear another interesting fact about the Civil War?" Bob asked.

"No!" they cried in unison.

"Listen, I'm just trying my best to enlighten the unwashed and uneducated masses," Bob continued. "Hey, ya'll will like this, and I swear it is absolutely true. Seems there was this retired major from the Virginia militia, one Wilmer McLean, who claimed the Civil War started in his dining room and, get this, he said it ended in his parlor."

"Ah, come on Bob," said Matt. "Don't you have something cooking in the back you need to attend to?"

"Not until you order something," Bob said. "Really, McLean was living in the middle of the first battlefield when the Battle of Bull Run was fought, in 1861. A confederate general was using his home as his headquarters. McLean later moved to Appomattox, and Lee signed the surrender papers in the parlor of McLean's home, which was near the Appomattox Court House. I swear, it's true! So, like the man said, you can look it up on—"

"No Bob, don't you dare say it!" screamed Lindy.

Mike smiled and picked up a menu. "I think we better order before it gets any deeper around here," he said.

Mike ordered a Muffuletta, the infamous New Orleans sandwich invented by the Central Grocery in the French Quarter. Pam ordered a Reuben and Matt and Lindy split a Dirty Bird.

"What's that?" asked Pam. "I don't see it on the menu."

"Well," said Matt, "Just think in terms of a Thanksgiving Day dinner. It has everything in it including the cranberry sauce. The only things missing are the mashed potatoes and filling."

"Filling? You mean the *stuffing*," said Lindy, smiling at Matt.

"No, darling, I said, and I meant, the *filling*," said Matt, smiling back.

"Okay girlfriend, and boyfriend, what you both mean is the *dressing*," said Rose, smiling at them both.

"You know," said Matt, looking back at Lindy, "the help around here has really gone to hell in a hand basket."

"Oh, good God, here we go again," said Bob from behind the counter. "Every time you two order a Dirty Bird, we have to go through the same song and dance. I think I'll just stop serving the darn thing, at least to you two."

"Lindy," said Mike, "Pam was telling me, and I didn't know this, that you and Matt met in high school, just like the two of us. So, your family moved from Cuba to the U.S. back then?"

"Oh, no. My folks sent me to live with my father's brother and his family in Indianapolis and I attended high school there. They and my brother had no intention of ever moving from Cuba. Remember, this was well before Castro. The plan was for me to study in the states, become proficient in English, then return and attend The University of Havana, which I eventually did. In the meantime I met this guy," she said nodding towards Matt, "and it really messed up my family's master plan."

"I still don't get it. You're in Havana, this guy," nodding towards Matt, "is in Indianapolis, so—"

Matt raised his hand. "I'd just like to interject, if I may, that my name is Matt, not *This Guy,* and thank you all for your consideration."

Lindy smiled and blew Matt a kiss.

"So, *this guy*, Matt and I, had fallen in love in high school. I was living with my aunt and uncle in Indianapolis and would return home to Cuba at the end of each school year. Matt would work for most of each summer, save enough to visit us in Cuba, and come down for a couple of weeks before school started in the fall. After high school, he headed off to college and I stayed in Cuba and enrolled in Havana University. But that didn't last. We were in love," Lindy breathed a deep sigh, placed both hands over her heart, blinked her eye lashes rapidly at Matt, then leaned her head back, making a swooning sound.

Everyone at the table applauded Lindy's theatrics.

"And still are, I might add," Matt responded, blinking his eye lashes rapidly and covering his heart with both hands.

"Oh, good grief, please stop, or I won't be able to eat my lunch," Mike said.

"Sorry," said Lindy. "Anyway, I returned to Indianapolis to my aunt and uncle's, and enrolled in Butler University. We became engaged and got married at the beginning of Matt's senior year at Wittenberg, in Springfield, Ohio. Our plans were to return to Cuba and start a business. Matt had fallen in love with Cuba—we even honeymooned there, and decided that's where we'd like to live. But this was back in what we call the Good Old Days, B. C., *Before Castro*. Fidel and his gang messed those plans up big time, along with, excuse me, screwing up the entire country."

"So your parents left after Castro took over. Did they have trouble getting out?" Mike asked.

"Well, they had to leave, no matter what it took. It was obvious to everyone by then that Castro was a communist and a dictator, just the opposite of what he proclaimed when he was in the mountains fighting the revolution. Then, in the Sierra Maestra mountains, he had promised a 'democratic revolution,' but, of course, it was all a big lie. My folks paid a high price to get out, but they couldn't remain in Cuba living under his dictatorship."

"If it's not too personal, what do you mean by a "high price,'" asked Rose, who by now had pulled up a chair and joined the table. The lunch crowd had cleared out and even Bob, leaning on the counter, was listening to Lindy's story.

"It's not too personal. At that time my folk's were in their early forties, and in most respects, it was a tough decision. Some family members believed in the revolution and decided to stay. But my folks didn't, and as a consequence, left the family, gave up their entire life savings, their home, a beach house they had worked hard for, and virtually everything else they possessed.

The revolutionary government confiscated it all and in return, gave them passage on the last Red Cross ship that left the island. By then, each city block in Havana had a communist block leader, and the block leader where my folks lived came to their home the night before they were to leave. She took an inventory of everything in the house, including the number of teaspoons in the kitchen drawer. Would you believe it? She even listed the can of lard in the refrigerator! Can you imagine that? After the inventory was taken, my folks were given the government's permission to leave. They arrived in Miami the next day on the last Red Cross ship to ever leave the island. They had the clothes on their back, five dollars in my Dad's pocket and a tooth brush.

"Wow, when was this, Lindy?" asked Mike."

"The spring of '63."

"So they came to live with you?"

"Right, in Indianapolis."

"Okay Lindy, you're not going to believe what I'm about to tell you, and I don't know why I never thought to tell you until now."

"What's that?" Lindy asked.

"*Naughty.* Believe it or not, she actually played a little role in Cuba's history."

"What? Get out of here!" Lindy said, an astonished look her face.

The statement caught everyone by surprise.

"She was there, in Cuba, in Havana. In fact, several shrimp boats from here, and South Carolina, are all part of that history."

"'My gosh, this is incredible. I never heard any of this," said Lindy.

"Well, here's the deal," said Mike.

All the other customers had left. Bob came from behind the counter, switched on the florescent "Closed" sign, walked over to the table where the others sat, placed a pitcher of iced tea on it, and pulled up a chair.

"A few years later, long after your folks had left, it was somewhere around 1980 or 1981 as I recall, some of the shrimpers from here, and all along the North and South Carolina coast, were participants in the Cuban Mariel Boatlift."

"Oh, I'm very familiar with the boatlift," said Lindy, nodding her head.

"It was something else," continued Mike. "Castro and the U.S. government made an agreement to let thousands of Cubans leave the island. Most people realized the reason Castro went along with the deal was because Cuba's economy was in free fall and near collapse. My Dad was part of the boatlift and spent several weeks there on *Naughty*. He'd pick up dissidents who wanted to leave the island and delivered them to Key West and Miami. Willy was with him, but he wouldn't let me go, said there might be trouble and I was too young."

"You're right Mike, it was 1980. Over 125,000 Cubans were transported by the flotilla over several months from Mariel Harbor, in Havana, to Florida. Of course Castro, being an S.O.B., took full advantage of the agreement. He opened up the jail cells and released hundreds of criminals, and also crazies and terminally-ill people, along with purging the island of any political opposition and anyone else who didn't go along with his *revolucion*. But, at least they got out safely. Prior to that boatlift, many people had risked their lives, and many even died, trying to leave. God, that seems like an eternity ago."

"Well, it was," said Matt. "And *Naughty* and Mike's dad, were a part of it. I can't believe how all this came together! Cuba, New Jersey, the revolution, Indianapolis, Baltimore, Varnamtown, Holden Beach, and here we all sit today enjoying fine fare in Archibald's Deli. Amazing, truly amazing."

"It is, but enough of the philosophical stuff and onto the lighter side of life," said Bob. "You guys just reminded me of something. I've been thinking about adding the Cuban Sandwich to our menu. Tell you what, let me work on it and sometime next week we'll have this same distinguished panel of gourmands reconvene and give it a taste test. We certainly have a couple of experts here."

"Sounds great to me," said Lindy, "but I'll tell you, it'll be hard to top this Dirty Bird you make."

❦

They were about through with lunch when Matt looked out the window and saw Willy pull into the parking lot and scamper out of his pickup.

"Darn it, we should have asked Willy to join us," he said.

Willy hustled through the door and walked directly to their table.

"Pull up a chair Willy, if want you can have half of my Muffuletta, I can't finish it," said Mike.

"What's a Muffuletta?" asked Willy.

"Well, now I know you need to try it. Sit here next to me."

"Listen," said Willy, grabbing a chair, "the reason I'm here is that . . . Mike, you must not have your cell phone with ya."

Mike patted his pockets. "Ah, you're right, I left it in the truck. Why, what's up?"

"Well," said Willy, "I'm almost scared to tell you this, but Billy Bodean is trying to get a hold of ya. You didn't answer your phone, so he came by the dock where Tommy Lee and me was working on *Naughty*. I heard you mention you was coming here, but I didn't want to let him know where you were."

Mike laid his sandwich back on the plate. "Thanks, Willy. Well, this can't be good," he said, looking around at the group.

"Wouldn't hurt anything to call him back," Pam said.

Although she hadn't spoken a word about it since the fire, Mike knew that Pam still had thoughts of becoming a wealthy lady.

95

"Lindy, could you or Willy give Pam a ride home? I want to see the ass . . . the gentleman in person, and Matt, it would probably be a good idea if you went along with me."

"Hold on a second Michael, before I decide on that, promise me you'll behave," said Matt. "I don't want you, or me, getting in trouble."

Mike looked Matt straight in the eye and raised his right hand, palm out and showed four raised fingers. "I'll behave, scout's honor."

"Mike, you were never a boy scout."

"How could you tell?"

"Forget it, let's go."

Matt and Mike got up from the table and headed towards the door.

Willy sat looking at the half of the Muffuletta sandwich which Mike had placed in front of him. He opened it, and stared at the contents.

"Okay," he said looking up, "which one of you lovely ladies is gonna give me a clue as to what I'm about to eat?"

CHAPTER 19

"You haven't seen or spoken with your favorite realtor since the day we were in his office?" asked Matt.

"Nope."

"Have you and Pam talked any more about the situation?"

"Nope."

"Have you given it any more thought?"

"Nope."

"It's a dead issue?"

"Yup," said Mike, never having taken his eyes off the road during this brief exchange.

"I admire a person of few words and firm convictions," Matt said.

Matt and Mike were in Mike's black Chevy pickup headed for Varnamtown and Billy Bodean's office.

"Really," Matt continued, "I think it's noble of you to stick to your guns, but man, that's one hell of a lot of money."

"You think I don't realize that? But damn it, Matt, money can't take the place of some things. We live in a home that my dad built. That means more to me than all that friggin' money. I'm a shrimper, and I'm proud as all hell of it. I enjoy the life. I know who *I* am, who *we* are, and I like who we are and I want to stay who we are. We enjoy our friends, hell no, we *love* our friends! The truth is, some are closer than our own family. I've known most of 'em since we were little kids playin' hide and seek on the shrimp boats! Okay Matt, listen, here's the deal, and believe me, I've thought it all the way through."

It wasn't difficult for Matt to see that Mike was getting pretty worked up.

"Say I sell the property," Mike continued, "and we move someplace, someplace like Holden Beach, for example. I'm telling you it just wouldn't be the same for Pam and me. It'd be like starting over in some foreign country, one where it's fun to visit, but you really don't want to live there. And there's this . . . if I did sell, and then bought or built another place in Varnamtown, since everyone would know we're loaded, I know it'd affect some folks. Maybe not on the surface, they wouldn't admit it, but I wouldn't be a shrimper any more, I wouldn't belong. I'd be this hot shot, rich guy. The relationships would change, you know what I'm saying? You see where I'm coming from?"

"I do Mike, I understand completely. I said a minute ago that you were noble, and I meant it. You're also a realist, a romantic, and a good man. I don't know what I'd do in your situation. I'd probably cave, take the money and run. Maybe not, and I hope to never be put to that kind of character test. I might not pass! Oops, looks like this is your lucky day, Michael. That's Billy Bodean's red Hummer parked out front."

There was a black Lincoln Town Car parked behind Billy Bodean's Hummer. "He must have a client. Maybe we should sit outside and wait," Matt said.

"That looks like the same car I saw at Archibald's," said Mike, "and we're not going to wait. I don't know what he wants, but it'll only take a split second for me to say 'no' to whatever it is, then get the hell out."

"Well," said Matt, as they exited the truck and headed toward the door, "to tell you the truth, the last few days have been a bore. No heart attacks, no fires, no politics of significance, no good looking chicks on the beach. Why do I get the feeling all that's about to change?"

Mike shook his head and laughed. "Not to worry Matthew, not to worry. We've got everything under control, including me. Quick in, quick out."

Entering the office, they saw that Billy Bodean, seated at his desk, had a flustered look on his face. Seated across from Billy Bodean was a younger man, thin, shaved head and wearing rimless glasses. He wore khakis and a black polo shirt. *Yankee* immediately flashed through Matt's mind and Mike immediately recognized him as the stranger who had held the door open for them just a short while ago at Archibald's.

Billy Bodean and Allen looked up as the two men entered. Billy Bodean's frown quickly changed into his patented, phony smile.

"Gentlemen, gentlemen," he said, "I've been trying to reach you, Mike."

"So I heard," Mike replied, "Willy told me you called."

"Allen," he said, turning to the stranger, "I'd like you to meet Mike Conrad and . . ."

"Matt, Matt Paskins," Matt said.

"Oh sure, now I remember," said Billy Bodean.

"How could you forget?" Matt said, smiling. "Particularly as I practically saved your life the last time we—"

"Allen is a business associate of mine from Chicago," Billy Bodean quickly cut in, not wanting Allen to learn the details of his last encounter with these two in his office.

Allen recognized Mike from Archibald's. "Mike and I met in passing a short while ago," he said. He also knew that Mike was the shrimper whose property D'Agostino wanted, and whose boat he had torched. Rather than suffer through Billy Bodean performing some meaningless song and dance, Allen decided to forego the B.S. and lay it all out.

"Mike, let's skip the bullshit, I know who you are, and

I'm sure by now you have some idea about me." Looking over at Matt, he continued, "I assume this guy is a friend of yours."

Mike nodded.

"I can speak frankly in front of him?"

Again, Mike nodded.

"Okay Mike, now that we know the terrain, let's get on with it. I'm the guy who's been attempting like crazy to buy your property through Mister Billy Bodean here."

"You've been trying to buy my *home,* Mike replied.

"Yes . . . well . . ."

"And you're also the bastard who torched my boat along with this asshole," Mike added, nodding towards Billy Bodean.

Allen looked back at Mike, an incredulous expression on his face. "I have no idea what in the hell you're talking about."

"Yeah, right." Mike took a few seconds in an effort to get his temper under control. "I'm certain that *Mister* Billy Bodean has told you more than once that my *home* is not for sale."

"He has, yes, several times in fact. I know he's been persistent. Now Mike, listen, you've been an excellent negotiator, I've got to give you credit for that. You've really strung us out on this one. But frankly, it's now time to dispense with all the crap. Excuse me for what I'm about to say," Allen said, almost chuckling, "but, Mr. Conrad, I really am about to make you an offer you can't refuse."

"What more do I have to say? I told you damn it, my property, my *home*, is not for sale," Mike repeated. "Not at *any* price! Why in the hell can't you people get that through your thick skulls?" He turned and headed for the door. His hand reached for the door knob.

"Two and a half million," said Allen, calmly.

Mike froze in place.

His, Matt's, and even Billy Bodean's mouth had dropped.

It flashed through Matt's mind that this was the second time in this same office that a nervous, apprehensive silence had swept over it and lingered. Time, indeed, had once again stood still.

Two and a half million dollars. It was an incredible sum, they each knew it. It was an unimaginable amount.

Matt stared at Mike, who had not moved a muscle. For a moment, it looked as though Mike might be in shock. He may well have been. Maybe he was having second thoughts. With so much money on the table, he'd be crazy not to reconsider. Who wouldn't?

Mike took his hand off the door knob and turned back to face Allen. He looked at Matt. He turned his head slightly and looked at Billy Bodean, whose mouth remained open. He slowly shook his head, turned from the group, opened the door and walked out of the office.

The silence was broken by Allen.

"I take that as a 'no," he said to no one in particular.

"Be my guess," Matt said, and followed Mike out the door.

Allen turned to Billy Bodean. "You can shut your damn mouth now. You want to know the truth, I wasn't authorized to go that high, but I had to assure myself that his position was firm. Now that we know that, we, you and I, are somehow going to have to do something about it."

"How we gonna do that?" Billy Bodean asked.

"Well, it looks like it's going to take something more than a fire now, doesn't it?"

◈

Back in the truck, Mike got behind the wheel, pulled out of the driveway and headed back towards Archibald's. "Maybe they're all still there," he said.

A couple of minutes passed before Matt spoke. "Seems to me the price of *nobility* just increased dramatically," he said.

101

"Might even say it just skyrocketed."

Mike looked over at Matt, then turned his head back to the road.

"Shit," was all he said.

CHAPTER 20

They had turned off NC 17 at the I-95 entrance, north of Savannah.

Matt and Lindy were headed for Miami to visit Lindy's folks who had relocated from Indianapolis several years earlier. With everything that was going on, this was as good a time as any to get away.

All indications were that Curt, without the satisfying aid of Cohiba cigars, was headed toward a full recovery. In an effort to lessen the frustration, Matt, on his evening visits, usually carried along a silver shaker of chilled, Bombay Sapphire martinis. Such thoughtfulness on his part had a profound, positive impact on the chief's attitude.

Mike Conrad's attitude had also shown considerable improvement. His efforts were now totally concentrated on bringing *Naughty* back to life. Gone were discussions of the fire, and of that last shock of an offer in Billy Bodean's office.

A real surprise, as it turned out, was Tommy Lee. Having spent much of his youth in the boat business with *his* father, the knowledge and experience he brought to the project proved invaluable. He and Mike could not get over the similarity of their backgrounds. They became fast buddies. Tommy Lee rose early each morning and arrived back home late each evening having spent the entirety of each day in Varnamtown working on *Naughty*.

They were relieved to see that Carlos knew his stuff, and were a bit surprised at the degree of professionalism he brought to the task of painting Tommy Lee's house. He was, in fact, doing a terrific job.

Maria and Bunny gave cooking lessons to each other based on their respective country's cuisines, and Bunny spent a great deal of time with Maria in discussion of, and shopping for, the soon-to-be-born baby. Bunny had decided it was best if Tommy Lee didn't know just how much shopping for the baby she and Tommy were responsible for.

So, before anything else surfaced that would hold them back, Matt and Lindy took off for the Sunshine State.

"Well, here we are dear ladies," . . . the statement included Satcha, who was nestled on Lindy's lap . . . "once again cruising along our favorite chunk of the Eisenhower Interstate Highway System," said Matt, shaking his head, "the dreaded I-95. Everybody hang on. Ya know, we can thank 'ol Ike for this, but I think if he ever saw the speedway this turns into approaching Miami, or the legendary backups heading into D.C., he might have scrapped the whole idea!"

"*You* dread it? Take a quick look at this. The trucks are scaring her to death. She's behaving like an ostrich."

Matt glanced over and saw that Satcha had buried her head across Lindy's breast and had tucked it under Lindy's forearm. Her tiny body was trembling.

"We got ourselves a wimp of a dog," said Matt, "but I can't blame her. We share the same feelings about I-95. Let's pull over and I'll tuck my head in there for a while, hmmm?"

"Matt, just keep your dirty mind and eyes on the road."

"Well, it was a thought. Let's do this. When we get to Jupiter, we'll turn off and take the turnpike the rest of the way in and avoid the insane frenzy into Miami on 95. I think some of those idiots believe the I-95 signs are the posted speed limit. Did I tell you I read in last Sunday's paper that in Barcelona, Spain, there's an auto accident every eighteen seconds? I'll bet Miami's got that beat by five seconds."

Matt was looking forward to this trip. He and Lindy enjoyed The Keys, but both considered Miami a second home. His relationship with Lindy's folks was terrific, and he felt very much a member of the family. His Spanish, far from fluent, was passable, but prone to the occasional error. There was, for example, the time he meant to compliment his mother-in-law on the fine meal she had prepared by telling her: "*Esta una buena cochina.*"

"Matt," Lindy had corrected him at the time, "the word is *cocinera,* not *cochina.* You just called my mother a good pig!"

This incident was possibly surpassed by a church service, delivered in Spanish, they had attended in Miami. At one point Matt understood the minister to have asked everyone to stand. Matt stood, heard some giggles, looked around, and noticed he was the only man standing. The minister had acknowledged all the mothers in attendance on that Mother's Day Sunday. Oh well.

After an overnight in Melbourne, they continued on the turnpike the next morning and arrived in Miami during the noon hour.

"Let's grab a bite before we check in or see my parents," said Lindy.

"Sounds good to me. How about a Cuban sandwich at

Larios?" Matt asked.

"Great. I wonder if Gloria Estefan still owns it. Rumor has it she owns half of Miami."

"I wouldn't doubt it," said Matt, "the lady has done well, and she sure as hell can sing. Beauty, brains and talent, hard to beat."

Lindy cleared her throat.

"Fortunately, I married just such a woman."

"Nice recovery," Lindy said.

The sandwich was, as always, excellent, with some fed to Satcha as the three sat in the air conditioned car.

"Bob's Cuban sandwich turned out awfully good," said Matt, thinking of the new menu item at Archibald's.

"It did," said Lindy, "the only real difference is in the bread. You just can't find true Cuban bread north of Florida and I've never understood why."

They headed for La Quinta. The inn accepted dogs, and was located within walking distance of Lindy's folks condo. During previous stays, Matt would frequently walk the two and a half miles to the condo complex.

The 750 mile drive to Miami was, in many aspects, similar to journeying to a foreign land. Matt would go for extended walks, shop, dine out, and visit relatives and during it all, hear little to no English spoken. He even kept his car radio tuned to the Spanish music stations and streamed them on his iPad. As soon as he hit Miami, he became immersed in the Miami/Cuban culture. Life on Holden Beach was akin to living in Paradise, but Miami held a special intrigue for him. The people, the food, and the music resulted in the perfect trifecta. Then, if one wanted, and Matt often did, there was the big city stuff such as the opera, the symphony, museums, Broadway shows, even a jazz joint or two. What was there not to like?

Years earlier, with Fidel's Communist revolution and the shock of the Cuban exodus into southern Florida, many believed

Miami would suffer an economic catastrophe from which it would never recover. Quite the opposite had occurred. At the time of the Cuban influx, Miami was in an economic tailspin, its future bleak. The Cuban tidal wave, although creating severe problems, over time, revitalized and saved the city. Today, Miami is a destination location. One report indicated that it now had more visitors annually than New York City. In no small way, this was the direct result of the Cuban influence in both its local and international business affairs, and its vibrant cultural climate.

Matt and Lindy spent the first few days seeing relatives, chatting with Lindy's folks and frequenting favorite restaurants. Toward the end of their trip they would take the time to stock up on favorite food stuffs that were unavailable back home.

Lindy's family was large. All those members who wanted to leave Cuba had fled the island one way or another over the years. Some wound up in Spain, others were spread around the world. Most however, came to Florida, and Miami in particular. There were a few who believed in the revolution and had chosen to remain. One became a high-ranking official in Castro's government. It was recently mentioned that he'd finally come to realize he had been living a lie for fifty years. But at this point, there was little hope of his leaving the island and starting a new life in a new country.

At least once a year, Matt or Lindy would concoct a totally irrational excuse to treat themselves to the Sunday Champagne Brunch at the luxurious Biltmore Hotel in Coral Gables. It was an event, a highlight of the year for them. The hotel, with its Mediterranean motif, was in keeping with its lush Coral Gables residential setting. The Biltmore's Sunday Champagne Brunch is considered among the most celebrated and lavish in the country. The price tag might also be considered a tad lavish by some, but Matt and Lindy had convinced themselves it was worth every penny, or, more realistically, every dollar. So, as in the past, it was just a matter of which one of them offered the most creative excuse. This time, it was Lindy.

"Matt," she said on the third day there, "it's been ages, simply been *ages*, my dearest, since I've had a *decent* caviar with my Eggs Hussard."

The time prior to this it had been Matt who had offered: "Darling, I've found it most difficult to enjoy steamed shrimp these days without sipping a perfectly *proper* Champagne cocktail, don't you know."

The required reservation was made and that Sunday they drove up the arched driveway and delivered their car to the uniformed attendant.

Walking through the spacious lobby, with its high ceilings and marble columns, Matt turned to Lindy. "Hon, I can't explain it, but every time I walk through here, I feel I've been transported to some luxurious, grand European hotel. Not that I've been to that many grand, European hotels, but this place, in Miami of all places, reeks of what must be meant by 'Old World Charm.'"

"I know," said Lindy. "I get the same vibes. Look at that ceiling. I don't know how high it is, but it's way up there and each of those frescos is hand painted. It's just so beautiful."

They walked across the beige, Italian limestone floor, again marveling at the lead glass fixtures, the carved mahogany furnishings and the lush vegetation. They stopped at one of the two nine-foot high, mahogany and inlaid brass bird cages. Each large cage contained brightly colored, nesting wrens. The bird's lunch had just been prepared and placed in their cages. It consisted of various fruits and seeds which had been carefully laid out in intricate, colorful, floral patterns at the base of each cage. Each food presentation was a work of art.

Matt looked at Lindy. "I've really seen it all now," he whispered. "You think our sparrows would appreciate something like this? Bet the cardinals would love it."

Lindy elbowed him in the ribs.

They walked downstairs to the open-aired Fontana

Courtyard and were immediately escorted to a very good table; a *good* table being defined by Lindy as one which gave her an unobstructed view of the Miami elite who had come to eat. People watching, for Lindy, had been cultivated into an art form and was a top, if not *the* top priority, when brunching at the Biltmore.

Matt's immediate objective after being seated was to enjoy a couple glasses of champagne as a prelude to the fine dining experience they were to savor.

A trio of musicians in the far corner of the courtyard played soft, acoustic, Latin- inspired music. The tropical plants and flowers throughout the courtyard were in all their splendor. All was well within this perfect, peaceful, luxurious world.

After the initial flute of champagne, and after an over indulgence of prime beef, eggs of every preparation known to man, steamed shrimp, caviar, sushi, king crab legs, smoked salmon and other epicurean delights, it was time of the chocolate mousse and a final glass of champagne when Matt heard Louie Armstrong singing *What a Wonderful World.*

He removed his cell phone from his shirt pocket. "It's Mike."

"Hey Mike," he said, holding the phone in one hand while picking up his spoon with the other and eyeing the chocolate mousse.

"Matt, how you two doing?"

"You wouldn't believe me if I told you. Let's just say I'm about as close to heaven as you can get."

"I'm afraid to ask for details, so I'll just take that as good," said Mike, laughing. "Hey Matt, listen, I just got off the phone with a guy from Miami who's got a couple of old shrimp boats dry docked along the Miami River. I told him what I was looking for, and it looks like he's got some stuff I could use. I'm gonna take a run down and have a look. You got some idea where I can stay?"

Matt hesitated, then said, "I'm in the middle of something Mike, and don't get any raunchy ideas. I'll call you back in five minutes."

"Great, but I gotta tell you, my imagination is running wild," laughed Mike.

Matt took a spoonful of mousse, closed his eyes, hummed, "Mmm," then smiled and looked over at Lindy. "Mike's coming to Miami to look for some parts for *Naughty*. What'd you say I call him back and ask him to bring Pam? I'm familiar with the area he needs to get to along the Miami River. Mike and I can do that, then the four of us can spend a couple of days frolicking about in Miami."

"That's a good idea Hon, I like it, but, we can't short shift my folks."

"We won't. I remember your Dad telling me that, when they were still in Cuba, he'd take some vacation time from the bank each year and go out with the shrimpers; he loved the ocean. He and Mike will hit it off, no question. It'll be great. After what Mike and Pam have been through, they deserve a fun break."

"They do. Go ahead and call him back."

Matt made the call and filled Mike in on his and Lindy's plan.

"Damn, I should have thought of that! What a great idea! Getting away from here for a few days might just be what the doctor ordered. I'll tell Pam to start packing and go over what I need done here with Willy. Matt, this is terrific, thanks."

"Okay," said Matt. "Call me with your flight info."

"We're on," he said, looking at Lindy and giving serious consideration to a return visit to the dessert area.

He started to get up just as the waiter arrived with their check. He gave it a knowing glance, smiled at Lindy and pulled the credit card from his wallet.

"More caviar, sushi or champagne before we sink further

into the abyss of financial ruin?" he asked.

"Oh no, my love, I've had an elegant sufficiency, any more would be an abundancy."

Matt laughed. Growing up, if someone had the audacity to say, upon completion of a meal, that he or she was *full,* or even worse, God forbid, utter those dreaded words, *I'm stuffed,* that person would receive an intense laser stare from his mother, followed promptly by the *elegant sufficiency* lecture. No one who experienced it would ever forget it. And certainly, no one who experienced it, would ever again pronounce that she or he was *full* or *stuffed.*

"Well, another incredible brunch at the Biltmore, and ya know, taking everything into consideration, the price isn't at all out of line," Matt said.

They had left the table and were waiting for the valet to deliver the car when Matt heard Louis singing on his cell phone again.

It was Mike. They had booked a flight for that evening.

"I know it's quick Matt, but I got a great deal on the tickets. I hope the timing is okay with you guys."

"Terrific! I'll make the hotel reservation and we'll pick you up. And Mike, as far as a deal, you know you could be a millionaire tomorrow by just scribbling your name on a few pieces of paper."

"Whoa Matt, there's to be no more discussion about that. Please don't bring it up again while we're there. It's over. It's done. It's history."

"Right," Matt said, "Got it."

They hung up.

Matt shook his head as he pocketed the phone. He had a strong sense that somehow or other, it was far from over. It was just a matter of time before the other shoe dropped. He was almost certain of it.

CHAPTER 21

"You're where?"

"Miami."

"Miami? Fucking Miami, as in Florida?"

"Right Jock." Allen could feel the heat coming through the cell phone.

"What, let me guess! You had this uncontrollable urge to see the Dolphins play, right? No, wait, you don't even watch football for Christ's sake. Wait! Wait! I got it! You're on the beach and you're sipping mojitos, and you're watching the broads parade their lovely, bikini clad asses! Is that it? What in the hell is going on with you Allen? Miami! You're supposed to be in fucking North Carolina!"

"They're here."

"Whose there?"

"The shrimper and his wife, and those friends of theirs I told you about."

"What in the hell are *they* doing there?"

"The shrimper is checking out some parts for his boat."

"Shit," Jock replied.

"I'm staying in the same hotel and keeping a close eye on them."

"Shit."

"Jock, an opportunity might present itself."

"Shit."

There was a pause.

"Okay, that's it Allen. That's enough. Contact Pipo Herrera."

"Herrera? Why?"

"Ain't it evident?"

"Jock, listen, I can handle things. There's no need to bring the Miami guys in."

"Yah, you've done just great so far. I'll call Herrera myself."

"I don't see how he can help, Jock."

"You don't see how he can help? For Christ's sake Allen, he controls Miami, shit, he controls Florida, Georgia and Alabama! Get with him. He likes the idea of the development. I'll call you back."

"Okay, Jock."

"And Allen, stay off the beach. I don't need you going bonkers over some hot, little bimbo showing her ass off to you down there."

"Right, Jock."

Shit, Allen thought, as he closed his cell phone.

CHAPTER 22

Allen followed the shrimper's gang of four in his rented Town Car to the International Mall on NW 12th St. He watched as they parked their car and headed into the La Carreta restaurant. Allowing a couple of minutes to pass, he left his car and followed them in. Once inside, he was surprised by the size of the place. It was much larger than he had anticipated, with several separate, but open rooms, each room jam packed with tables and people, and each busy with hustling waiters, waitresses and bus boys. The next thing that struck him was the noise level. It was loud, very loud. It appeared that absolutely everyone in the place was talking, and at a fevered pitch at that, but no one was *listening*. He'd never seen, or heard, anything quite like it.

Standing where he could get a decent look into each room, he spotted where the four from North Carolina were seated.

Allen asked for a corner table where he could keep an eye on the group. Certain that with his New York Yankee's baseball cap, large sunglasses, Miami Dolphins sweatshirt, and khakis shorts, he was safe from being recognized by either of the two men. Even so, it was best to keep a safe distance.

The busboy placed his silverware, rolled in a napkin, and a pitcher of ice water on the table. Unfolding his napkin and looking around, it dawned on him that he was hearing no English being spoken. None. Not a word. *Well,* he thought, *if I'm ever going to get an authentic Cuban meal . . ..*

"Sir?"

Allen turned his head, and in a word, was dumbstruck. He was being handed a menu by one of, if not *the* most gorgeous creature he had ever laid eyes on. Shiny, jet black hair fell loosely to her shoulders. Radiant green eyes shone like the finest of gems. Brilliant white teeth, behind sensuous, full red lips formed a smile any model would envy. The white, off-the-shoulder blouse revealed just enough to drive Allen's brain into a tail-spin.

Recovering as best he could from a momentary loss for words, this lawyer, this wordsmith, this person who depended upon his proficiency with the English language each and every day, came up with his best professional response . . .

"Huh?" he asked.

She continued to smile as she offered him a menu.

He took it from her without giving it a glance as he remained transfixed by the vision of loveliness standing before him.

"Would you like something to drink while you look over the menu?" she asked.

As she spoke, Allen detected the slightest of accents. God, it was charming.

Regaining some degree of composure, and now smiling himself, he started to ask, "How did you know—"

"How did I know to speak to you in English and not Spanish?" she asked.

"Right, what gave me away?"

"Maybe it's the combination of the ball cap and shirt, or the shorts. I really can't say, but you have *gringo* written all over you," she laughed.

"Hmmm. Well, now that you found me out, what drink do you suggest this *gringo* have?"

"If you've never tasted one, we make a fabulous mojito . . .

115

rum, mint, lime and soda water . . . it's wonderful."

"Sold," he said, and handed the menu back to her.

"Oh, aren't you going to dine with us?" she asked.

"Of course," he said, embarrassed, still a bit flustered by her beauty. He took the menu back.

She smiled, and turned toward the bar area.

He watched her walk off. He had never, ever seen such motion. It wasn't that the walk was exaggerated or even that obvious, it simply had the most suggestive rhythm, the most subtle undulation, an implied sexuality that had Allen's mind thinking thoughts that were anything but subtle or implied. Thoughts that if acted upon, could land him in serious trouble.

He glanced over to the table of four. They appeared to be having a fine time with much animated conversation and laugher going on. He was envious. It had been a long time since he had enjoyed an evening such as the one he was observing. Why? What in the hell was happening with him?

The vision returned with his mojito.

"Made your mind up yet?" she asked.

"Well, no. To be honest, this will be my first Cuban meal. How about some help? Any suggestions?" As he spoke, he removed his sunglasses and looked directly into her eyes. *God.* He had never seen such a beautiful shade of green. For a fleeting moment, their eyes locked on one anothers.

"You might try our Vaca Frita," she said quickly, unsure of what had just happened, but knowing full well he had no idea what she was suggesting.

"Vaca Frita?" he asked, shifting his eyes to her cleavage.

"Yes, in English it would translate to "Fried Cow."

"You gotta be kidding . . . fried cow," he said, still on the cleavage. Was that a tiny dimple? Yes. Were there others just beyond—

"No, really, that's what it means," she said, now beginning to have some fun. "Or perhaps you'd like to try, "Ropa Vieja," which, before you ask, in English would be "Old Clothes.'"

"Sounds delicious," he said, laughing, and going back to the eyes which now just happened to be sparkling like two well-polished emeralds.

"Okay, seriously," she said, "since this will be your first Cuban meal, I'd suggest "Lechon Asado," which is roasted pork in a special marinade, and comes with black beans, rice and platanos maduros. And for dessert, you must try our flan. It's the Cuban's most traditional meal, and we do it all very well here."

"Sold again," he said, having little idea of what he was about to eat, but already anticipating her walk away from the table.

He wasn't disappointed. He watched in amazement, or was it ecstasy, as she headed back to deliver his order. *Good God, what in the hell's going on with me?* He looked at the pitcher of ice water. *Maybe I should just dump it over my head,* he laughed to himself. *Well, at least Jock shouldn't be too pissed,* he thought. *She isn't some beach bimbo in a bikini.*

She returned with his drink, placed it before him and said she'd return in a few minutes with his dinner.

He again watched her walk off. *Holy Mary Mother of God, I've never seen anything so sensual in my entire life..*

Heading back to the kitchen, the waitress was trying to figure this guy out. He was dressed like a geek, no, more like a klutz, but there was something about his manner, his way of speaking, that suggested the attire didn't match the man. Thank God he'd taken off those silly sunglasses. If he'd take off that ridiculous hat he'd probably be a rather good looking guy. And he had a sense of humor, which she appreciated in a man. And there was that brief moment of intensity she saw in his eyes. She guessed they were about the same age. He might be a couple of years older, possibly early thirties. Intriguing for sure.

At the table, he took a sip of the mojito. *Nice, very nice.* He'd have another with his meal. *Was she married?* He hadn't noticed a ring. He'd make it a point to look when she came back. That, and he hadn't even bothered to look at her name badge. Let's face it, it was what was the mounds behind the name badge that had grabbed his attention.

He glanced over and saw that the meals were being served to the four *amigos* from North Carolina. Still a lot of chit chat and laughter. *Lucky people, well, at least for the time being.* He started to look away when Mike's friend Matt, removed his cell phone from his shirt pocket. Allen watched as Matt's smile turned to a frown. He watched as Matt began to slowly scan the dining room. Allen put his sunglasses on. He watched as Matt looked directly at him, then continued with his scan. When Matt had finished his survey, he smiled, then laughed, nodded his head a couple of times, and placed the cell phone back in his pocket. He watched as Matt rejoined the table conversation. It was nothing. He was mistaken. No problem.

Allen decided not to make a move on this incredible creature until he had finished dinner and she brought him the check. When she returned with his meal, he noted that there was no ring and that her name was Joan. Joan. Didn't sound very Spanish to him.

The roasted pork was good, outstanding even. It was instantly a new favorite dish. The pork and a third mojito gave Allen the heady feeling that luck had come his way in this boisterous place. All he had to do now was get his act together and smoothly, or was it suavely, make the perfect pitch. Well, what the hell, he was a slick-talking Chicago lawyer, right?

"I hope you enjoyed your meal," she said as she picked up his dessert plate and placed the tray with the tab on the table.

"Everything was terrific, really. Thanks for your recommendations. Between the food and the mojitos, it couldn't have been nicer. But now, please pardon my brashness, but I've gotta ask, your name is Joan?"

She flashed another drop dead smile. "Not very Cuban,

huh? Well, my dad's a gringo. He was born and raised in Chicago. He met my mom, who is Cuban and born in Havana, on a business trip here to Miami. My full name is Joan Esther Diaz Rodriguez. Is that Spanish enough for you?"

Good God, what a terrific break!

"I'm from Chicago, and I'm a business trip same as your dad! What a coincidence! Joan, this is my first time in Miami and I've heard some terrific things about this city, particularly South Beach. But I *really* need someone who knows it well to show me around. Could you see yourself free to—"

"I'm really sorry, but it's a strict company policy . . . we are not permitted to socialize with customers," she said. Her fabulous smile faded as she spoke.

"Could you make a one-time exception? I swear, I'm a decent guy that you can trust and I know we'd have a terrific time. Please, reconsider."

She picked up the tray containing the tab and his charge card without saying another word, and left the table. He, instinctively, shook his head and stared in wonder as she walked away. If no one had been around, he might have banged his head against the wall behind him. Had he blown it? Was she miffed at his pass? Had he come on too strong? *I'm losing it,* he thought.

Walking back to the cashier, she noticed that he had given her his black American Express Centurion card. *Oh my,* she thought. She was familiar with the card. Her dad had one. She knew it was made of titanium and was offered to select and extremely wealthy customers on an invitation only basis. As she recalled, it had something like a two hundred and fifty thousand dollar limit, give or take. Clearly, this gentleman was well off and not the klutz his attire would suggest. *What's going on with this guy?*

Waiting for her return, he drummed his fingers on the table. What else could he say? He had to see her again, there was no two ways about it. No women had ever affected him like this. Other than the fact that he was going nuts, something was happening to him that he liked, that he liked a lot. All thoughts of the screwed-up Carolina land deal, of Jock back in Chicago, and of that idiot realtor in Varnamtown, were millions of miles away. He was feeling good, really good, for the first time in a long, long time.

She returned shortly, placed the receipt tray on the table, gave him a quick, courteous smile and walked away before he could say anything more to her.

Damn, he thought, *that's it. I blew it.*

He looked over at the table of four. They were gone.

Shaking his head at how quickly things had changed from quite terrific to quite lousy, he picked up the pen and started to sign the tab. It was then he noticed a slip of paper sticking out from under the receipt. He slid it out.

In beautiful, clean, crisp lettering, there was a number, a phone number. And just below that number was a drawing.

Joan, the half Chicagoan, the half Cuban, the complete vision of loveliness, had drawn a "smiley."

CHAPTER 23

"Willy, it's still hotter than hell down here."

Sweat was pouring off them both. It was early evening and they'd been working on the engine all day with just a quick break for a lunch that Bunny had prepared for the two of them.

"That's for sure," said Willy, handing a wrench to Tommy Lee. "I'm not certain Mike is right about fixin' up ol' *Naughty*. There's just too much that ain't right with 'er."

"Well," said Tommy Lee, "we can't blame him for trying. Unfortunately, the more time we spend down here, the less I'm certain we can repair the damage. I'd hate like hell for him to have to buy a new engine but . . . hey Willy, move that light a little closer so I can see what I'm doing with this connection. When I'm finished with this, we're calling it a day. And then my good man, it's ice cold brewskis time!"

"You got that right!" said Willy. "But," he went on, "I gotta tell ya, even if we do get 'er goin', by the time she's ready, there probably won't be *any* makin' money out of shrimpin', or even fishin' for that matter."

"How's that?" said Tommy Lee.

"Well," said Willy, "some of the fellas was complainin' more than usual a couple of days back. Seems some damn, new government regulation just come out that's gonna make it damn near impossible to make a living for sure. Some fish, I forget which one it is this time, has been added to the illegal list. The hell of it is, they can't catch the legal ones without catching some of the illegals. So if they get caught with the illegals on board, which they know they can't keep, they can be fined a ton of money, might even lose their license. Damn it, Tommy Lee, the damn government regulations are gonna kill us. They're gonna put us all out of business. We're just skimpin' by as it is."

"Sounds like what they call a 'catch 22' Willy. You guys are damned if you do, and damned if you don't. What you're saying is that if you get caught, even though you're trying hard to fish within the regulations, the fines could put you out of business. If you don't take the chance, you're out of business."

"You got that right, but it ain't just the business, it's our lives, ya know. It's what we do. How we gonna survive if the government keeps up with all this, well, all this shit?"

"I don't know. I really don't know. It's a bitch for sure."

"It's been getting to be a bitch for a while now. I've heard 'em all complainin'. Thank God I don't own a boat or a fish house, I couldn't handle it. Listen to this, and you ain't gonna believe it. When some outfit, say like Captain Pete's, or Varnam's, buys fish to sell, or crabs, or clams, there's some kinda form they gotta fill out. It's called a trip something or other. Anyways, they have to do it each time they buy stuff. On this form I'm talkin' about, they've gotta write down the license number of the boat they got it from, his dealer number, his license number, how many crew were on the boat, the gear the fisherman used to catch the fish, when the boat left out, when he unloaded, the body of water he caught the fish in, where he caught 'em, along with a list of the types of fish and how many pounds of each. Now ain't that all a crock of shit?"

"Willy, tell me you're not serious. He has to do this for *everything* he buys from a commercial fisherman?"

"Yup, it's the honest ta God's truth. He has to legally show, in writin', where every damn shrimp, every damn crab and every damn clam and every damn fish came from."

"Man, I had no idea."

"Yes sir, and somewhere in Raleigh, there's this big damn warehouse bustin' its guts with tons and tons of forms that I'll betcha not one damn person's ever looked at. But, that's the law and we gotta do it. Sorta pathetic, huh? And like I told ya, it's getting worse. The regulations are suffocatin' us."

"Sure sounds like it."

"All these guys wanna do is be able to keep their boats afloat and their nets wet. Seems simple, don't it?"

"It does, and that's a neat way to put it. Tell you what, Willy, I'm ready for that beer. I'll grab 'em outta the cooler in my car. We'll have a couple, then I've gotta get on home."

When they emerged from the engine room, Willy took a look at Tommy Lee and burst into a laugh.

"What? What's so funny?" asked Tommy Lee.

"Well, you sorta look like you just come out of a West Virginia coal mine!"

Tommy Lee looked down. He was covered with soot and grease. He looked over at Willy and smiled.

"Hey, partner, if I look half as bad as you, Bunny won't let me in the house!" He laughed and headed off for the beer.

When Tommy Lee returned from his car, he lifted two bottles of Yuengling out of the cooler and handed one to Willy, who was standing on the dock having a smoke.

"It's been a good day, Willy, we got a lot done."

Willy lifted his bottle. "Listen, it's always a good day when you're looking at the flowers and not the roots!"

"That's good, I like it!" said Tommy Lee, laughing. "You're just full of it today. Hey Willy, you heard from Mike since he and Pam left for Florida?"

"Nah, I don't expect to. Between searching out parts for *Naughty* and hooking up with Matt and Lindy, they'll be pretty darn busy. Oh, speakin' of that, did I tell ya that a couple of nights ago I was over at Paradise Cafe having a few beers when some guy comes in and starts talkin' with me and the other fellas at the bar? He was askin' if any of us knew a Captain Mike Conrad. Says he's got important insurance information he's gotta give Mike concerning the boat. I told him Mike and his wife was down in Miami trying to find some parts for *Naughty*."

Tommy Lee's antenna went up.

"You tell this guy *where* they were in Miami?"

"Nope, truth be told, I couldn't remember if I had to. I'd had a few beers by then. Told him I thought it was some kind of Mexican joint, but that's all."

Matt had earlier told Tommy Lee that he and Lindy would be staying at a La Quinta because of their new pup. Chances were good Mike and Pam would have joined them there. How many La Quintas could there be in Miami? If this guy, whoever he was, wanted to track them down, it wouldn't be difficult. Tommy Lee didn't know if Mike had insurance on the boat or not, but something about what Willy had just said didn't sit well with Tommy Lee. It didn't pass the smell test.

"Willy, think back to the other night and tell me what else this guy said and what he looked like."

"I didn't say nothin' wrong, did I?"

"Nah, Willy, I'm just curious."

Willy gave Tommy Lee a description, as best he could remember, of how the conversation went and what the guy looked like. It wasn't much.

"Okay Willy, thanks. Sounds fine by me. Listen I gotta run or I'll be in serious hot water with the lady of the house. What's say we get an early start tomorrow."

"For sure. See ya here," Willy said, still bothered that maybe he had said something he shouldn't have.

When Tommy Lee got seated back to his car, he took out his cell phone and tapped in Matt's number.

CHAPTER 24

"Yeah, now I remember you. We met in Vegas a few years back," said Tio Pipo Herrera. "Jock told me you were coming along pretty good, but at this particular moment you needed some assistance on a little situation you got."

Allen and Tio Pipo were seated in one of the interior courtyards of Tio Pipo's Spanish-style mansion located in an exclusive section of Coral Gables. Allen had been cleared through a security gate, then cleared again, including a pat down at the entrance to Tio Pipo's elegant home. It was mid afternoon and a maid had just delivered a pitcher of sangria and wine glasses, and placed them on a glass patio table between the two men.

"All the stuff in here is fresh, of course," said Tio Pipo, picking up the pitcher. "Great afternoon drink, hope you like it," he said as he filled the two large wine glasses, wiggling the pitcher a little to make sure some of the fresh fruit fell into each glass.

"I'm sure I will," said Allen, reaching for a glass. "Had my first mojito last night at dinner. I'm basically a wine and scotch guy, but mojitos are now way up on my list. This looks good. Did Jock fill you in?"

"Here's to ya," Tio Pipo said raising his glass. "Yah, he did and he sounded pissed, bottom line being that this fisherman, or whatever, ain't convinced he needs to sell his place."

"That's it. Did he tell you what we've tried so far?"

"Yup, sounds like you've got one stubborn son-of-a-bitch on your hands."

"'Fraid so."

"Okay, so he's what, here in Miami, right?"

"Right, along with his wife and another couple . . . close friends of theirs."

"He got any kids?"

"Nope. Got five or six dogs and their "kid" if you will, was the shrimp boat. That's how we thought we could get to him."

"Doesn't leave much to work with."

"Nope," repeated Allen as he picked up the pitcher and refilled both glasses. "Good stuff." He placed the pitcher back on the table.

"Just the women," said Tio Pipo.

Allen shot a look at Tio Pipo. "I'm sorry?" he said.

CHAPTER 25

After a couple of hectic days of giving Mike and Pam a first-class tour of Miami, including dinner at La Carreta and another at Joe's Stone Crab in South Beach, along with lunch at El Palacio de Los Jugos and at Lario's, Mike and Pam understood Matt's and Lindy's fondness for Miami. There was not only a lot of fun stuff happening, but Mike and Pam had quickly turned into a couple of Cuban cuisine foodies. In fact, Pam was loading up on Cuban cook books and Cuban canned goods. As much stuff as she'd bought, she'd have to ship a goodie box back to Varnamtown, maybe two.

By the third day, Mike needed to get down to business and check out the boat parts he needed. The ladies had no interest in going to the Miami River with the men, so they were dropped off in the morning at the corner of Lincoln Road and Collins Avenue, where they could begin their quest of shopping the entire length of the infamous Lincoln Road shops. This had been a difficult decision to make as they also wanted to hit the Miracle Mile, in Coral Gables. Both locations had shops that could do serious credit card damage. Lindy leaned toward Lincoln Road, as she had become more familiar with it over the years and knew something of its history. As she explained to Pam, it was originally envisioned as a counterpoint to Fifth Avenue in New York, and

Rodeo Drive, in Los Angeles. Although falling short of those lofty aspirations, it had some wonderful stores, restaurants and cafes. Several had outdoor seating which allowed for even better ogling of the beautiful people at play. An extra added attraction, unavailable at the Biltmore, was that the beautiful people here were often accompanied by their unique, designer dogs.

The men dropped the girls off at the corner of Lincoln and Collins where they then walked over to Washington, where the mall began. Lincoln Road at this point, was no longer a road, but had been filled in connecting the two sides forming an open air mall. Stores and restaurants, including many outdoor restaurants and cafes, lined both sides and stretched for several blocks to Alton Road.

Coming out of a dress shop, Lindy said, "Let's run back to that cigar store we passed. I want to pick up a couple for Matt. I've been there before and we can watch them actually roll the cigars. Supposedly, the tobacco leaves are grown from Cuban seed, and, of course, the workers are all Cuban."

While they watched the cigars being rolled, Lindy jotted down a short note. As they left the store, she slipped the note into the Ziplock bag containing the cigars.

They decided to sit for awhile and have a drink, and maybe some lunch. They settled into chairs under a large blue awning at the Cafe at Books and Books in front of the Books and Books store.

"This is by far my favorite Miami book store," said Lindy.

"Well then, I guess I'll just have to check out their cook books after we have lunch," said Pam.

"You keep this up and you'll have more Cuban recipes than I do," Lindy said, "and I'm the Cuban in case you've forgotten!"

"Well, Mike's gone crazy over the stuff. We both thought it would be like Mexican food, but it's far from it. It's a lot more, umm, subtle I guess is the word—great flavors, but it doesn't knock you over. Anyway, I just want to take a look in the store."

Determining the need for a "pick-me-up" to get them through the remainder of the spree, they each ordered a large daiquiri.

The waiter returned and placed their drinks on the table.

"Good God, I've never seen a glass this big," said Pam.

Holding her drink with both hands, Lindy raised her glass.

"Here's to good friends, good food and *great* shopping," she proposed, holding the glass high.

"You betcha!" Pam said, raising her glass and laughing.

Seated at far edge of the outdoor cafe, three men had settled in. Two were wearing white guayaberas and had ordered the traditional small, but strong, Cuban coffee. The third man wore a New York Yankee's baseball cap. He also wore a concerned look on his face. He had ordered a mojito.

He looked over at the two ladies who were, plain to see, having a ball, while he sat there with these two goon *companeros,* each drinking coffee and running their mouths in machine-gun like Spanish with him not understanding a damn word. Not that he cared. He didn't give a damn what they were saying. Leaning his head back and tossing down a good slug of the mojito, he realized, for certain, without question, at that moment, that his life had turned to shit. His relationship with Jock was all but gone. His job, wait, what job for Christ's sake? He didn't even know what in the hell his job was anymore. Aside from all that, the basic fact was that he was depressed. Fun times were non-existent. He couldn't remember the last time he'd had a good laugh. And most troubling, he was currently on an insane mission for Jock that could result in serious harm to, what he now considered, some decent folks, not to mention putting himself in danger. It was a far cry from what he had signed on for years ago.

Take today, for example. Here he sat at an outdoor table somewhere in Miami, with two strangers, two Cuban thugs, who, he was certain, were speaking in Spanish just to piss him off. He'd heard them earlier speaking perfectly acceptable English with barely any trace of an accent. Cuban Mafia guys, whose boss was connected with Italian Mafia guys, like his boss, who was probably connected with the Mexican Mafia and the Russian Mafia guys. *Damn, I wonder if the Swiss have a Mafia,* he thought. He took another swallow of the mojito, shook his head, and stood up.

"Gotta make a call," he said, and walked away from the table. He glanced over at the two ladies who were, by his count, on their second drink. *Nice. Fun. Good for you. Enjoy the moment.*

He took out his cell and hit the redial button. This was his fourth or fifth try for the day.

"*Hola,*" answered the voice.

That was close enough for Allen to know it meant hello.

"*Hola,* Joan," he said, feeling hyped at the sound of her voice. "This is Allen, remember, your favorite customer from yesterday?"

"Hmmm, let me think. Ah yes. I had one customer yesterday wearing a pair of the most incredible, god-awful, really, really tacky sun glasses matched only by his entirely mismatched wardrobe. I'm guessing that'd be you."

"That'd be me and I know I looked like a real jerk. Sorry. But, how'd you know it was me?"

"Well, and I mean this, it wasn't your attire. I've never given out my phone number before. Never. It was a matter of elimination, and to be honest, believe me, I'm still not sure why."

"Hmm, well, thanks. I think. Joan, I'm calling because I was serious about that city tour thing. Could you possibly find time in the next few days to show me around?"

"I can't believe I'm saying this because it really is against company policy, but yes, I'd like to do it, but on one condition."

"What's that?"

"You won't dress so goofy."

"You got it," Allen laughed. "In fact, you can watch me throw everything in the dumpster."

"Oh, you can keep the stuff—just don't wear it all at the same time again!"

They chatted a while longer and made their plans. He hung up and returned to the table feeling a million times better than when he had left it. Finally, something *wonderful* was happening. He felt on top of the world. He even cracked a smile. Hell, if he knew how, he would have whistled.

Approaching the table, he heard the two thugs chatting in English, but switching to Spanish as he got closer. *Assholes,* he thought.

He considered ordering another mojito, but saw the two ladies rise from their table and head toward the book store.

The men paid their bill and waited for the ladies to reappear. Once they did, the men followed at a discreet distance.

After ducking in and out of a few shops, Lindy and Pam crossed Jefferson Avenue. They were now close to Alton Road, which ended the Lincoln Road shopping area. Both had arms laden with bags from several stores. The plan was to buzz the men, then walk back and be picked up where they had been dropped off in the morning.

When they entered a dress shop near Alton Road, one of the two goons took out his cell phone and placed a call. A minute later, Allen heard the familiar sound of the Beatles singing *It's Been a Hard Day's Night* and reached in his shirt pocket for his phone. It was Tio Pipo.

"You like to read?" he asked.

"Of course I do Tio, but—"

"You see where that store, Books and Books is?"

"Yah, we were just at their cafe a few minutes ago."

"I'll be waiting for you inside the store."

"But—"

"Now!"

"But—"

The call went dead.

CHAPTER 26

Lindy and Pam had finally reached Alton Street. Standing on the corner, they looked at each other and sighed. Between the two of them, they had made quite a haul.

"My arms hurt," said Pam.

"Well, it's the price we serious shoppers must occasionally pay, but look at all these great deals! And think how much we saved the guys with all the stuff we bought on sale!" said Lindy.

Pam grinned. "Did you see the deal I got on those red shoes? I can't believe it! Nine ninety-five! I should have bought a couple more pair!"

"They are awfully pretty," said Lindy. "I wonder if you clicked the heels together if you'd wind up in Kansas," she laughed.

"Who in the hell wants to go to Kansas!" squealed Pam.

Well, they both thought that remark was about the most hilarious thing they had ever heard and laughed 'til tears ran down their cheeks.

"Hey, we did good lady. We came, we saw, we conquered!" declared Lindy.

"Not bad for a girl from little 'ol Varnamtown, North Carolina," Pam said, stretching out the southern drawl. "I've never bought so much at one time. Oh my, Mike'll go berserk!"

"Oh, no, he won't. He'll be glad we had so much fun. And just think, we're not done! Tomorrow it's onward and upward to Coral Gables and the Miracle Mile!"

At this point, a couple of giddy teenagers would have had nothing on these two.

"I've gotta call Matt," Lindy said, bending down and placing her bags on the sidewalk. She looked in her purse and found the phone.

Pam stood by, still grinning from ear to ear.

"Here, let me help you with those bags lady," said a stranger who had suddenly appeared by Lindy's side. He leaned down and quickly ripped the phone from her hand.

"What the— we don't need any— and give me back my—" Lindy gasped as the stranger showed her the pistol inside the pocket of his guayabera. He kept the pistol pointed at her face as she tried to straighten up.

A second man had his pocket pressed against Pam. She didn't have to be told that it too, contained a gun.

"Grab the rest of those bags," the first one said to Lindy.

She had no sooner gathered them in her hands, when a white, four-door limo swept up beside them.

"Get in. NOW! Move it! No noise or you're both dead!"

Pam whimpered as a car door opened and she was shoved into the limo.

A small, bag fell to the ground as Lindy was pushed into the back seat, bumping her head against the top of the opening.

The men jumped in on either side of Lindy and Pam, squeezing them tightly to the center. Doors slammed closed. The tires of the limo screeched as it sped away.

⌘

Allen didn't like it. He hustled back to Books & Books

knowing that something was going down, something that didn't include him. He'd lost all control of the situation. *Damn.* He hurried through the short alley that led to the store and looked in.

Damn. The book store had six or seven different rooms. As quickly as he could, without actually running, he made a fast tour and glanced in each room. Nothing. No sign of Tio Pipo Herrera.

He got his cell out and began speed dialing Tio's number, thought the hell with it and left the store. He quickly surveyed the area. No Tio Pipo. He turned toward Alton Street and starting jogging.

He was half a block away when he saw the two women being hustled into a white limo. He hollered, waved his arms and broke into a run. The limo was out of sight by the time he reached the corner.

Panting heavily, he bent over, gasping for breath. He noticed a small white bag resting against the curb. He picked it up and, looking inside, saw three cigars in a Ziplock bag. He removed a hand written note.

Hey Hon,
Know you'll really enjoy these on our front porch.
(I'll stay inside.)
Love,
Lindy

Allen shook his head. He hadn't been told that this was how it was going to go down. Today was only supposed to be surveillance.

The bastards were using both of the women.

He stood for a minute with the bag in his hand, thinking.

It was there, standing at the end of the Lincoln Road Mall in South Beach, Miami, on a bright, clear, sunny day, that Allen Skubic made the decision that would change his life.

❦

Allen kept the bag and walked back to the shopping area. He wasn't sure what to do, what his next step should be. He started to call Tio Pipo Herrera again, then Jock, then decided the hell with calling anyone. He sat down in the same chair where he had been with the two goons only a few minutes earlier. He called the waiter over and ordered a mojito. He had to figure what in the hell was going on and why he hadn't been included in the plan.

It's Been a Hard Day's Night sounded through his pant's pocket. He removed the cell and looked at the I.D. It was Jock.

"Jock, damn it, what in the hell's going on? A couple of Tio's guys just nabbed the two women off the street!"

"Yeah, he called."

"Where are they?"

"I don't know. I didn't ask—don't want to know. I trust him. They'll be okay for the time being."

"Why wasn't I filled in on this?"

"We both thought it best for you to be out of the loop and let his guys handle the not so pleasant stuff. That way you're clean. Listen, I'm gonna need you in a couple of days. I'm not sure when and not sure where, but stay put in Miami 'til I get back to you. And Allen, remember what I told you earlier about those beach bimbos; hands off those cute little asses!" he laughed.

"Sure, Jock."

Funny, Jock, Allen thought as he closed his phone, *you're really quite the card.*

CHAPTER 27

Seated at an outside bar along the Miami River, Matt and Mike had finished their fish sandwiches and were nursing a second frosted mug of Heineken. It was a perfect Miami afternoon with the temperature somewhere in the mid seventies, a slight breeze coming out of the south and a perfectly cloudless Florida blue sky. The trip to the river had panned out great for Mike. He'd located several essential parts for *Naughty,* made the buys, and arranged for shipping, all of which had him in terrific spirits.

"It's been a good day Matthew, in fact, a great day. I can't thank you enough for your help."

"Anytime Michael," Matt said, draining his glass, "always glad to be of service."

"Pam and I were just talking last night about how much we enjoy hanging out with you guys."

"The feeling is mutual Mike."

"One thing we noticed is that you and Lindy never seem to get upset with one another. There are never any cross words between you two."

"Oh, believe me, we have our moments. You just haven't been around at the right time," laughed Matt. "But honestly, it's been a great ride so far. In fact, it's been terrific. We realize we've been pretty lucky. But I can't help but think of something I read the other day. It went something along the lines of , "The last word in an any argument is what the woman says. Anything a husband says after that, is the beginning of another argument."

"Oh my, that certainly has a ring of truth to it," Mike laughed.

Mike looked at his watch. "I thought we're hear from them by now. It's going on three. They've had more than enough time to max out the cards."

"They have," said Matt. "It'll take at least half an hour or so for us to get back to Lincoln Road, and we sure as hell don't want to get caught in five o'clock Miami traffic—biggest mess you'll ever see."

"I'll give Pam a buzz," said Mike, pulling out his cell.

He waited until Pam's message kicked in.

He looked over at Matt. "No answer."

"I'll try Lindy."

Matt waited. His call went to Lindy's message.

"I don't understand, one of them should have answered."

"Let me try Pam again," Mike said.

As he was redialing, Matt redialed Lindy.

With concerned looks, they sat staring at each other.

"Something's wrong," Matt said, shaking his head.

"Maybe they shut off their phones and went into an old historical church or something," said Mike.

Matt shook his head again. "I don't think so, not today. They had shopping on their minds, not touring. They probably had a toddy or two at lunch, but something's not right."

"Let's go, I'll keep trying both numbers," Mike said.

They paid up, rushed to the car and headed for Lincoln Road.

❧

"Shit, there's no place to park," Matt said, turning his head back and forth looking for a spot. "It's *always* like this here!"

Twice they had driven by the corner of Lincoln and Collins where they were to pick up the ladies. Mike was still trying to reach them by phone.

"Over there on the left, someone's backing out!" shouted Mike, pointing to the other side of Collins.

Matt whipped the car around before anyone else could grab the spot, and quickly backed in. The two men hurried out of the car and glanced at the parking meter.

Matt had a quick flashback to the first time he had used one of these damn meters in South Beach. It took a lifetime to read the instructions. He recalled seeing other visitors standing in front of the meters staring and shaking their heads. At that time, it was funny, watching people trying to figure the damn things out.

Time had expired on this one, and now it wasn't at all funny.

"I forget how these damn things work!" Matt said. "Screw it, let's get going." They began jogging back toward Lincoln Road.

"You take one side and I'll take the other. Check inside each store. And check the tables out front just in case they're out here gabbing and not paying attention to the time," Matt said. There was panic in his voice.

They started their search. They were quickly working their way through the area, poking their heads in each store and restaurant, and scanning the outside tables.

Mike was about to enter a ladies apparel shop when he froze in place. *No. No way!*

He turned, squinted his eyes and looked back. He couldn't get a clear enough look. The man's back was to him now.

He ran over to Matt, who was two doors up on the other side. He grabbed Matt's arm and spun him around.

"Jesus Matt, we gotta hurry!"

"What? You see the girls?"

"No, damn it, I saw something else! There's a guy up ahead we gotta catch!"

Matt stopped and turned to Mike. "What are you talking about?"

"Just keep walking, we gotta hurry. Listen, remember that guy we met in in Billy Bodean's office? That cocky-ass lawyer who said he had an offer I couldn't refuse?"

"Yeah sure, why?"

"That's him up there, the one walking towards Collins wearing the black baseball cap and sweat shirt."

"I don't see—okay got him! What makes you think it's the same guy?"

"I gotta pretty good look. Matt, I'd swear to Christ it's him!"

The guy stopped for a moment, turning to look in the cigar shop window, giving Matt a better view.

"Shit, it does sorta look like him. We gotta get closer."

The man turned away from the shop and started back toward Collins.

"Pick up the pace," Matt said. "Hurry!" They weren't fast enough.

As they drew close, the man they suspected of being the lawyer they had met in Varnamtown, was at Collins Avenue. He raised his hand as a taxi pulled up and he slid in.

Matt and Mike both started running and hollering for the cab to stop, but the driver pulled away from the curb.

"God damn it!" cried Mike.

Matt, doubled over and trying to catch his breath, looked over at Mike. "This is no coincidence," he muttered.

"Damn, damn, damn," said Mike. "They're in trouble, Matt! Shit! What in the hell do we do now, call the cops?"

"I don't know—maybe. But what in the hell do we tell them? Our wives are missing and we saw someone wearing a baseball cap and sweat shirt who we think is involved, but we don't know who he is or where he is?"

"We could call Billy Bodean and get the guy's name."

"Shit, he's in on it Mike. He's part of the deal! And I don't trust that son-of-a-bitch. He'd only make it worse. Let me think."

"The cops could check with the cab companies," Mike said.

"Mike, I don't know the law, but I know there's some kind of waiting period before the cops will declare a missing person situation. I think it's something like twenty four hours."

"Well, what in the hell are we going to do?"

"Damn it, I don't know!"

Matt stood thinking for a few moments, shook his head, then reached in his pocket and pulled out his cell.

"Who ya calling?" asked Mike.

"I hate to do it, he sure doesn't need any stress, but I'm calling the only person I know who might be able to help us," Matt replied.

CHAPTER 28

After resisting the temptation to pick up a couple of hand rolled, Cuban cigars, Allen caught a cab at the corner of Lincoln and Collins. As much as he would have enjoyed the smokes, after the way this day had gone, the last thing he needed was to reek of cigar smoke when he showed up for his highly anticipated date with Joan.

As the cab pulled away from Lincoln Road., Allen tried to relax. He leaned back, closed his eyes and rested his head on the back seat. He had a lot on his mind. As days go, this one had been pretty lousy, having started off in the company of two idiot Cuban goons, followed by the kidnapping of the women. The two ladies—where in the hell were they now? One minute they were having a ball shopping, the next minute they were snatched off the street by Tio's hoods. The thought of their being harmed filled him with remorse. Allen had a sinking feeling. He was responsible. He had lost control over the situation with the North Carolinians. Tio Pipo and Jock had stepped in, taken over, and were now pulling all the strings. He, Allen Skubic, was out of it.

He, Allen Skubic, would now try his damndest to get things right.

But for the moment, he had to put this mess temporally behind him. There was no way he would allow the events of the day to screw up the only bright spot in his life. This evening he would dine with Joan, the stunning waitress extraordinaire. She had suggested meeting at a French restaurant, and his anticipation of seeing her again set him on an emotional high. He laughed to himself as he realized he hadn't been so excited about a date since high school.

The restaurant, the Versailles, sounded pretty fancy, but Joan had suggested he dress casual, not as casual as yesterday she had chuckled, but nonetheless, casual.

After yesterday's necessary, but obvious clothing fiasco with Joan, his attire for the evening took on an abnormal degree of significance. Returning to his room at La Quinta, the first thing he did was open the closet door and peruse his options. After a lengthily contemplation, he removed a stripped Oxford shirt, a pair of clean, pressed khakis, and a navy blue blazer, all of which he laid out on the bed. He'd wear loafers, no socks.

Satisfied with his selections, he removed a can of Heineken from the mini-bar, changed into his swimming trunks and a Chicago Cubs t-shirt. He took the elevator down to the lobby and grabbed a pool towel at the front desk, then headed for the hot tub. A half hour there, followed by a power nap and a shower and he'd be all set for the delightful, gorgeous, incredible Joan Diaz . . . whatever, whatever, whatever the rest of her crazy beautiful name was.

He had wanted to pick her up at her place, but she had insisted on meeting at the restaurant. Not the most positive of beginnings, but it was a start of what he hoped to be more pleasurable events to follow.

∗∗∗

Entering the Versailles, Allen immediately realized two things: first, if it was French, it sure didn't look it, and he certainly wasn't hearing any French being spoken, and second, it sounded every bit as noisy and loud as La Carreta had the day before. It was, he realized with some disappointment, another Cuban restaurant.

He looked around for Joan and saw she was already seated at a table. She spotted him at the same time, smiled and waved.

As he was being seated she said, "You look very nice this evening, Allen, quite a departure from yesterday. I like the new you."

"Thanks," he said as he looked around, "I thought this place would be French."

"Far from it," she said. "The Versailles claims to be the most popular Cuban restaurant in the world, and with some justification. It's the center of Cuban political activity here in Miami. Politicians come here to get support from the Cuban community, and when anything of importance happens with the Cubans, here or in Havana, this is where the media comes to get the inside scoop. This is the hub. Most presidential candidates make it a point to stop here to secure the Cuban American vote."

"Wow, quite a place . . . and may I add, quite loud."

Joan laughed. "Allen, before we go any further, there are three things you should know about us Cubans."

"Oh my, I guess I want to hear this! Shoot."

"First, when we are talking, we are not screaming at one another, although it might appear that way, it's just simply the way we talk. And it's not uncommon to see two of us talking simultaneously to each other, loudly, at the same time. Second, it's been proven that we are the fastest speaking people in the world, and I mean the entire known world."

"Well, from what I've seen and heard, I can certainly vouch for the first two. I can't wait to hear the third."

"Well, number three has yet to be proven, but it's a fact nonetheless. We Cubans know everything."

Allen stared at her. "Everything?"

"Yup, absolutely everything. If you have a question, or want to know anything about anything, anything at all under the sun, just ask a Cuban."

"Wow . . . so each and every Cuban has this sorta built in Google gene, is that right?"

"That's it, exactly!"

"My, I really like that third one, and now I definitely wish I were Cuban! By the way, before we go any further, you look positively stunning." He meant it. Joan had her gorgeous black hair swept back in a pony tail, was wearing a bright yellow, off-the-shoulder blouse, sported large matching, looped yellow earrings and, as he had noticed while being seated, white skin-tight Capri's.

"Why, thank you," she smiled. "Listen, this place is busy as usual, so let's order and I'll—"

"Hola, Joan, *como estas*?"

They both looked up.

Standing beside the table was a handsome, middle-aged gentleman with a tanned, weathered face and an impressive head of wavy, gray hair. It was a face that implied wisdom combined with authority.

"Good evening Your Honor, how are you?"

"Fine, Joan, just fine. I didn't mean to intrude, but I haven't seen you in awhile."

"We've been pretty busy at . . . ah . . .work," she replied.

"I see. How's your dad?"

"Doing just great, thanks."

"Wonderful! Tell him I said 'hi.' Listen, as usual, I have people waiting and have to run, but be sure and give my regards to both your folks, okay? Good seeing you again Joan," he said, leaving the table.

"Looked like an important guy," said Allen.

"Ah, actually, he is. He's, ah, the mayor."

"Of Miami?"

"Of course, of Miami! I would have introduced you, but he was obviously in a hurry. Listen Allen, there is something I—"

"Hi, Hon."

They looked up again.

This time, the gentleman standing alongside the table was wearing a neatly pressed black shirt with four gold stars on each collar, a black tie, a gold badge, and an insignia on each shoulder that identified him as police.

This time, Joan with a broad smile, stood up, threw her arms around the man and gave him a big hug.

Turning back to Allen, she said, with a somewhat embarrassed look on her face, "Allen, I'd like you to meet my brother. Roberto, this is Allen, a friend of mine from Chicago."

Allen stood and the men shook hands.

"Please, sit down," Roberto said, giving Allen a quick once-over. "Sorry I can't stay and visit, but I have to tell you, I highly recommend the pork chunks tonight Hon, they're incredible! I suggest you try to steal the recipe. Just don't get caught," he laughed. "I'd hate to have to arrest my favorite sister. Nice to have met you, Allen."

"Same here," said Allen.

"Thanks," Joan said, as the man turned and walked away.

Allen sat back in his chair, his arms folded.

"Oh, so that was Miami's Police Chief?"

"It was."

"He's your brother."

"He is."

"The one before was the Mayor, and apparently a good friend of the family."

"He is."

The waiter arrived at the table. They each ordered a mojito and for the entree, the pork chunks suggested by Joan's brother.

"Let's back up, you're waiting tables," Allen continued.

"I am, but I started to tell you earlier that I have a confession to make."

"Really?"

"My family is in the restaurant business."

"Oh?"

"Yes, we, ah, well actually, we own several here in the Miami area."

"Several."

"Right. When we met yesterday at La Carreta, I had just started my training. Let me explain," she said.

"No, no, that's okay, you don't have to explain anything."

"Well, I want to. You should know about me, and then you can tell me about yourself."

Their drinks arrived.

"You got me hooked on these," Allen said, raising his glass. "Cheers."

"There are much worse things to be hooked on," she laughed. "But let me finish," she said, sipping her drink. "I received my Doctorate in International Law, practiced a few years, wasn't happy with it and decided a few months back to join the family business. I want experience in each aspect of it, so I'm working my way up the ranks. After I spend some time waitressing, I'll work in one of the kitchens for a while, then purchasing, and so on. The only job I don't care about is parking cars."

Allen's head was spinning. Beauty, brains, money, obviously from a fine family, and the top cop in Miami for a brother.

"Your turn."

Allen wanted time to think. "Let's save that for a little later."

The waiter arrived with their dinner, and her brother's suggestion was spot on.

"I've never tasted pork this tender. The flavor is absolutely fantastic!" Allen said.

"That's because of the *mojo* marinade they use with the pork," she said.

Along with the black beans and rice, the plantains, and a

nice Chardonnay, it was turning out to be a perfect meal, with the perfect lady.

Well into enjoying the meal, Allen said, "Okay, so tell me about the plans for tomorrow."

"Not so fast! Your story first. Please, that's part of the deal."

"Well okay, if you insist," Allen said, and took a sip of wine.

"Here goes: I'm a mix of Swiss-German and we don't like to talk a lot, so this will be brief. We Swiss-Germans are smug, stubborn, thick headed, egocentric and tend to hide our emotions, and that's just five of our more outstanding attributes."

Joan threw back her head and laughed.

"We, like the Cubans, know everything, but unlike the Cubans," and here Allen raised his head and looked down his nose at Joan, "*ve* keep everything a secret so *ve* can feel vastly superior to every *vone* else."

Joan again threw her head back and laughed. "Oh my, this is ridiculous, now I'm really glad I'm Cuban!"

"Me too," Allen said, smiling. "Actually, if you insist on the rest of the story," he continued, "I'm a lawyer, and real estate is my forte. I'm a lifelong resident of Chicago, single, and never married. How about you, ever married?" he asked, raising an eyebrow.

She shook her head.

"I work for a private organization," Allen continued, 'and I'm in Miami checking out some properties for that organization. When I have time, I like to read. And I follow the Chicago Cubs, which, if you have any interest in baseball, tells you I'm also something of a masochist. So, that's my story and I'm sticking to it. Now, let's close the deal. Tell me about my private tour of your fine city after we leave here."

"Well," and here it was apparent she felt embarrassed as she fidgeted with her wine glass, turning the stem slowly as she spoke. "I only made time for dinner tonight, Allen. I thought if we somehow didn't hit it off . . . that, well . . . you know."

"I understand perfectly."

"Allen," she continued, "I can't tell you how much I regret having made that decision, but I've made other plans for the evening which I can't break. I'm really looking forward to tomorrow though, and I promise you a wonderful time."

Allen's heart skipped several beats. They chatted a bit more, realized they both were avid readers, that she was a rabid Marlin's fan, and so was aware of him having to be at least somewhat loony to hang in with the Cubs. Then they finalized their plans for the next day.

With everything in place, Joan reached over and gently covered Allen's hand with her own, and gave it a soft squeeze. "I'm really looking forward to tomorrow," she said, staring into his eyes. "Until then." There was another squeeze, and the most seductive of smiles.

She started to rise out of her chair. Allen got up, walked around to her side of the table and drew her chair back. It was the first time since meeting that he was close enough to get a whiff of her perfume.

He inhaled deeply and stared down at her, not wanting to forget the exotic fragrance of her body or the sheer headiness of the moment. He could live the rest of his life breathing in that intoxicating scent.

She got up, turned, and placed a hand on his shoulder. She looked into his eyes and for a moment he thought that she was about to give him a polite peck on the cheek. But instead, she smiled and softly stroked his cheek with the softest, barest brush of her fingertips.

"Until tomorrow," she whispered in his ear, then turned to leave.

Oh my God, this woman is going to drive me insane!

As she walked away, Allen couldn't help but notice the same alluring motion he'd first seen at La Carreta just the day before. He continued to watch as she stopped by another table and spoke briefly to yet another distinguished-looking gent.

What the hell, he chuckled to himself, *he's probably the damn governor of the state!*

Allen had never known such happiness; he was giddy with it. Good God, she had touched him, not once, but twice! Several years ago he was certain he had fallen in love, but nothing, absolutely nothing in the past compared to the sensation now burning within him.

He drummed his finger tips on the table. He sat, smiling, grinning, gloating, smirking, whatever the look is that someone head over heals in love does while sitting at a table by himself basking in the afterglow. He reflected on Joan's intoxicating perfume, which he considered quite exotic. However, upon further reflection, he changed his opinion. It was, yes, without question, *erotic!*

He again drummed his fingers on the table. He looked down at them. *This is getting to be something of a habit!*

He looked around and saw that no one was paying any attention to him. He poured what was left of the wine into her glass. *This is absolutely crazy!* He wanted his lips to touch hers, no matter how superficially. *I've lost it! Take me away and lock me up! Either I'm one very sick puppy, or I'm insanely in love. Whichever, I never want to lose this feeling!*

He shook his head. Of all the incredible, improbable things that could happen while on the road to discovering the girl of his dreams, there was her brother, Miami's Chief of Police! Could it be that what he earlier considered to be the *worst* couple of days of his life could turn out to be the *best* couple of days of his life?

He continued to drum his finger tips on the table. This time however, there was no question about. There was definitely a huge grin on his face.

CHAPTER 29

They knew they were on a boat, but that was the extent of it. After being forced into the limo, there had been an uncomfortable, painful car ride as they sat squashed between the two large thugs. They had been blindfolded, handcuffed and gagged.

Roughly shoved into a cabin of the boat, the gags and blindfolds were removed, but not the handcuffs.

After two hours on the water, with the boat constantly on the move, the cabin door was unlocked and opened.

In walked a very attractive young girl with shoulder length blond hair, dark blue eyes and a smile revealing extraordinarily white teeth. She had poured her body into a pair of skin-tight white shorts and a turquoise halter top that left nothing to the imagination. Even under frightening circumstances, it flashed through Lindy's mind that the blond hair came from a bottle, the blue eyes from contacts, the white teeth from excessive whitening and that this cute little thing had undergone a boob job of substantial proportions.

"Hi, I'm Ginger. Welcome aboard, ladies."

"Why are we here?" Lindy demanded.

"Like, I don't know. I was told you're the guests of my boss, and I'm supposed to see if you need anything, ya know?"

"Who's your boss and what's he want with us?" cried Pam.

"Like, you'll have to ask him that kind of stuff, ya know? Don't be upset with me!"

"Where are we Ginger?" Lindy asked.

"Well, you're on my boss's seventy-five foot Hatteras and like, a little while ago we were just off South Beach. Oops, maybe I shouldn't have said that. Well, I *can* tell you for sure that we're in the Atlantic Ocean," she giggled. "Would you like something to eat or drink? Like our chef, Ray, is totally awesome."

"No, we want to talk to your boss," Lindy insisted.

"Like he's not on board now," Ginger said. "Oops, I shouldn't have said that either. Darn it! You sure I can't get you something?"

"No," Lindy and Pam cried in unison.

"I'm sorry, I was just trying to be helpful, ya know?" Ginger pouted, as she turned and left, locking the door behind her.

Their cabin, actually a stateroom, was huge. Two large beds butted up against opposite walls. Earth tones with dark brown plush carpeting, beige walls and high gloss cherry wood dominated the interior. Very, very classy. A seventy-five foot Hatteras . . .

Pam sat on the edge of a bed and began to cry.

"The men will find us Pam, I know they will," Lindy said. She sat beside Pam and buried her head in her hands. She became aware, for the first time, of just how much her hands were trembling.

CHAPTER 30

"Curt, Matt."

Mike stood watching, hands in his pockets, as Matt spoke with Chief Everhart.

"Yeah, we're in Miami and we're in trouble. Lindy and Pam are missing. We think they were kidnapped by the guy who's been after Mike's property. We just saw him a couple of minutes ago, but couldn't get to him. Curt, we don't what in the hell to do! Should we go to the cops?"

Matt stood listening.

"No, don't do that. You can't travel yet and we might need you there."

Matt stood listening again, then said "Okay," and closed his cell.

"He says not to do anything until we hear from the girls or the bastards who have them. They're obviously using them for leverage. The cops can't help 'til we know something more."

"I don't like doing nothing," Mike said.

"I know, but we gotta wait for the call. No sense in hanging around here. Let's get back to the hotel, maybe someone left us a message."

❧

"Now we sit and wait," Matt said, letting the door to Mike and Pam's room slam behind them.

They sat on the beds, each holding their cell phone in their hands, staring at the blank TV screen. The prolonged silence was deafening.

"Shit," said Mike, as his eyes glistened with unshed tears.

CHAPTER 31

"So, you got the broads," Jock said, speaking with Tio Pipo, "any problems?"

"Nah, they're tucked outta sight aboard my little vessel."

"Tio, I've seen your little vessel. You could cruise the world in that thing!"

Tio laughed, "I have, twice! Listen, Jock, I haven't seen them yet, but my captain tells me they ain't teeny boppers, but they're decent looking enough to cause problems with the crew. Some of the boys can get a little, ah, ardent after a few drinks. You need to wrap this up."

"Don't let nothing like that happen! It shouldn't take but a couple of days to get it done."

"Just outta curiosity, what are you offering this guy . . . exchange the broads for the property?"

"Plus what I authorized Allen to quote him before, which was a mill and a half. He gets the wife, unharmed, and the money."

"You're getting soft in your old age."

"Yeah, well, I want this to go down legit and smooth so tell your captain to keep his boys in line. Also, we have this numb-nuts realtor in Varnamtown, North Carolina who—"

"Where?"

"Varnamtown. You ain't never heard of Varnamtown, North Carolina? I'm amazed Tio, a man of your vast travels and intellect—"

"Cut the shit Jock. The only thing I know about North Carolina is, ah, the Panthers, who are actually worse than the Dolphins, which is truly a difficult thing to comprehend, and what's that place with all the golf . . . Myrtle Beach?"

"Tio, Myrtle Beach is in fucking, *South Carolina.*

"See, I don't know shit."

"Okay, anyway, the numb-nuts realtor's got the paper work and we'll get him to Miami. I'm bringing the money. Allen is pulling it all together and we're counting on you for the logistics."

"You got it, but what if he still refuses?"

"Refuses! You kidding? The wives, the money—no way!

"A mil plus, huh?"

"Right, the last deal I authorized, plus the broads. Everybody walks away. We all walk away happy."

CHAPTER 32

Both heads snapped as they heard the lock click and the door being opened.

No one had entered the cabin since Ginger had been there earlier to remove the handcuffs.

"I know you said you didn't want anything, okay," Ginger said, as she pushed a cart through the doorway, "but that was like a while ago and I thought you might be hungry by now. I asked Ray, like he's the awesome chef I told you about, to fire up a couple of steaks."

She moved the cart between the two beds, lifted the lids off of two plates and revealed a couple of delicious locking filet mignons. There was also what looked to be a fancy version of scalloped potatoes along with broccoli in a yellow sauce.

"Like, I know I shouldn't have done this, okay" she said, turning her head toward the doorway to make certain no one was nearby, "but like, I thought maybe you could use this seeing how this isn't particularly a pleasure trip for you guys."

She reached under the cart and brought out two bottles of wine, one red and one white.

She then reached back under and brought out two wine glasses and a corkscrew.

"Would you believe it, but like my boss had this incredible

special room built just for wine, ya know? There's gotta be hundreds of bottles in it! Like, it's even temperature controlled!"

Lindy and Pam looked at each other. The truth was, they were hungry, and the wine would most certainly help calm their frazzled nerves.

"Listen Ginger," Lindy said, "we really appreciate what you're doing, but can you tell us why we're being held here?"

"I don't know," she whispered, "but like, I overheard the captain tell his crew to make sure you two stayed safe." She lowered her voice even further. "I don't like him, he can get nasty. But like, he knows he'll get in big trouble if he messes with me. Listen, I better get going, but call me when you're finished, okay, and I'll take this stuff away. It's sorta nice having a couple more women on board, ya know what I mean?" She left the cabin, locking the door behind her.

Lindy looked at the cart. "I think I'll start with the wine," she said. "You want white or red?"

Pam remained seated on the bed, and began crying again. "I can't handle this, Lindy!"

"Here," Lindy said, handing Pam a glass of wine. "Drink this, then I'll get you another. Really, it'll help, and Pam, somehow or other, we're going to get out of this mess."

Somehow we're going to get out of this mess. She repeated this to herself as she walked back to the cart. She picked up the bottle of red, looked at the glass, and took a long swig from the bottle. Then, another.

Somehow we're going to get out of this mess.

She put the bottle back down, walked over to the bed and sat next to Pam. She put an arm around her, drew Pam close, and began to rock the two of them slowly back and forth

Somehow or other we're going to get out of this mess.

CHAPTER 33

They could have taken the expressway downtown, but Joan decided Allen needed to see some of Coral Gables (he didn't mention he had been there) and little Havana, on Calle Ocho, for him to get a real feel for the Cuban influence.

Of course it made no difference to Allen. Just to be in this woman's presence was everything he needed. For all he cared, they could pull into a McDonald's parking lot and he'd be happy to just sit there dunking fries and gazing at her all day. Well, some things other than dunking and gazing did enter his mind. Joan was wearing the same erotic perfume he remembered from the evening before, and it was driving him nuts.

They drove by Maximo Gomez Park, otherwise known as Domino Park, where men sat at several tables, studying their next move. On their way to South Beach, they passed the Adrienne Arsht Center for the performing arts.

"I saw an incredible performance of *Aida* there, it was really quite a production. Do you enjoy opera?"

He didn't want to lie and say "yes," but he didn't want to disappoint and say "no."

"I prefer jazz," he answered.

Joan was thoughtful for a moment. "I guess I like both equally," she said.

My god, is there anything about this lady that isn't perfect?
On the causeway to South Beach, the brilliant blues and greens of the water impressed Allen, but what really grabbed his attention as they passed Star Island, were the many mansions, several with massive, multi-zillion dollar yachts docked in front.

"My God," he said.

"Nice, eh?" Joan said. "I think Gloria Estefan's place is there, and also Shaq O'Neal's. There's a bunch of famous folks; we can drive through if you'd like. It's gated, but it's public property so they sorta just give you a quick look and let you through."

"Nah, that's okay, I might be tempted to buy something."

"Right," she laughed.

Joan scooted over and wrapped her arm through Allen's. "So, what do you like best so far?"

"I haven't seen anything not to like," he said, "but I cannot tell a lie. My Miami tour guide is what I like best. Just being with you makes everything else perfect. I've never enjoyed a day as much as I have this one."

"Me too," she said, and squeezed his arm. "And the day is still young!" She snuggled closer and leaned her head on his shoulder.

The closeness of her body, the linked arms, the head on his shoulder and the scent of the intoxicating perfume were getting to the driver.

"Lady, if you keep it up, this car is gonna fly off the causeway and plunge into that gorgeous water below!"

Joan laughed, squeezed his arm again and gave Allen directions to get to the Art Deco district of South Beach.

"I had no idea," Allen said, looking at the colorful buildings, many of which were once homes, but now converted into hotels and motels. "Neat, really neat."

"Okay, now I want you to see our beach. Let's swing over to Collins Avenue."

Allen drove slowly along Collins. "It'll be nightfall by the time we find a spot."

"No, don't worry, it's always like this; we'll get one."

Within the next block, a car pulled out.

"See, I told you, we Cubans know everything!"

Allen pulled up and backed into the space.

He got out, opened Joan's door and walked over to the parking meter. He stood staring at it while shaking the loose coins in his fist.

In back of him, Joan was leaning against a light post and grinning from ear to ear.

He continued to jostle the coins and stare at the meter. She kept smiling.

Finally, in frustration, he turned and said, "How in the— then he saw her burst out laughing.

"It happens all the time," she said, "particularly with foreigners who can't read English. Just slide your credit card in, we'll need thirty minutes, punch that in, take the receipt and put it on the dashboard. Voila! It's done!"

"Some things are getting much too complicated," he said, while doing as instructed.

Finished with the parking meter operation, he took Joan's hand and the two of them walked along the sandy pathway toward the beach.

"Wow, it doesn't look quite like Lake Michigan. The colors of the water are incredible."

"I'm glad you like it," Joan said.

"Well, the water is beautiful, the beach is beautiful and having the most beautiful tour guide in all of the known world makes it the most beautiful day imaginable!"

"You tourist say the sweetest things," she said, looking over at Allen and squeezing his hand.

They took off their shoes, placed them on the beach and walked the water's edge, ankle deep, hand in hand.

They hadn't gone very far when Allen stopped, turned to Joan, slipped his arm around her waist, and placed a light kiss on her lips.

"I couldn't hold back any longer," he whispered.

Joan placed a hand behind Allen's neck and drew him down to her lips. Her's was not a light kiss. It was deep and filled with passion.

"I couldn't hold back any longer either," she whispered in his ear.

They broke their embrace when they heard the cheering.

Looking around, they saw a crowd of scantily clad bodies cheering, applauding and whistling.

Red faced, but smiling from ear to ear, Allen waved to the crowd as they hurried back, hand in hand, to pick up their shoes and get back to the car.

They were still laughing as they entered Joe's Stone Crab, just a few blocks away.

As usual, the place was packed, but they lucked out and were seated in the main dining room.

As the waiter approached, Allen asked Joan, "Wine, . . . a cocktail? What's the pleasure of the lady who just created a torrid scene on Miami's most famous beach?"

"It wasn't *that* torrid! You won't believe this, but after all that, an ice cold Presidente beer in a frosted mug sounds absolutely perfect to me."

"A couple of Presidentes," he told the waiter.

After the waiter left, Allen reached over and took Joan's hand. "This is really going to sound silly, but do you believe in love at first sight?"

Joan sat, deep in thought for a moment. "No," she said. "I believe in love at second sight. You have to remember how you looked the first time I saw you!"

"Oh, good grief, you're right," he laughed.

They reviewed the day, chuckled again at the South Beach

scene, never took their eyes off one another, and held hands across the table during the entire conversation. It was by now evident to both that something quite special was happening.

When it came time to order, they both went for Joe's Stone Crab Claws and Allen ordered an excellent Chardonnay with which he was familiar.

Allen was taking a sip of wine when Joan said, "Sorry, guess I'm sorta messing up your business plans."

"You gotta be kidding," Allen replied. "I've met the most incredible person I've ever known and am having the most wonderful time of my life! Business is the furthest thing from my mind."

"Have you even contacted an agent yet?"

"Yup, sure have. I'm working with a fellow by the name of Herrera, Pipo Herrera. Actually they call him Tio, which I understand means 'uncle.' Anyway, he's supposed to be one of the best real estate developers in southern Florida."

Joan had her wine glass halfway to her lips, but froze at the mention of Herrera's name. She slowly lowered it to the table.

"Say that again," she said.

"Say what again?" he asked.

"The name, the name of the person you contacted."

"Herrera. He's the guy my boss arranged for me to work with."

"My god, Allen, who do you work for?"

"I'm sorry, I don't understand."

"Do you have any idea who Herrera is?"

"Yes, of course. He's a real estate developer, and one of the best, at least according to my boss."

Joan stared incomprehensively at Allen. The words coming from this man, this man with whom she had fallen so madly in love, had her in shock. A wave of disgust swept through her body. She felt nauseous.

"No Allen, no." There was anger in her every word. "I can't

believe you're telling me this! Herrera is a crook!" She leaned over the table, hissing in a low voice. "But he's much more than that; he's a gangster, a mobster, he's slime, he's the king rat in the Cuban Mafia. My brother considers him the most dangerous man in the southeast. He kills people, or has them killed. He's a worm. I ask you again," she hissed through her teeth, "just who is your boss, and just who in the hell are you? You bastard!" She paused. A look of incredibility swept across her face. "You *knew* all along, didn't you! You already *knew* who Herrera was! My God, you *knew* who my brother was! You've been playing *me* all along!"

Joan picked up her wine glass and threw what was left of her wine into his face. She started to get up, but Allen grabbed her arm.

"Don't touch me!" she hissed, jerking her arm free of his grasp.

"Joan, do not leave! Let me explain. Please. This could be the most important moment in *our lives.*"

She remained across from him, her eyes ablaze.

Diners at the surrounding tables were trying hard not to stare at them.

Allen's mind was whirling. If he didn't get this right, if he tried to fake his way through it, it would all be over. He had to tell her absolutely everything, and then, when she had heard it all, every deplorable detail, he had to trust she'd understand.

"Can we go someplace private to talk?" he asked.

"No. I don't want to be alone with you. You scare me." She glanced at her watch, then back at Allen. "You've got five minutes."

Allen lifted the napkin from his lap, and wiped his face. He leaned over the table and lowered his voice.

"Joan, this may be more than a five minute-minute story. Some parts aren't so nice, you won't like them. But if I run over five minutes, don't leave. I don't want to lose you, I *can't* lose you. You hear the end, then make your decision."

Joan looked at her watch, then back at Allen. "Four minutes," she said.

CHAPTER 34

Later that same evening, off the Florida coast, Lindy and Pam were lying on their beds, each staring at the ceiling. There was knock at the door. Both shot up quickly, assuming it was Ginger, returning to retrieve the cart. They were wrong.

"Good evening ladies, this is your captain speaking." He laughed at what he must have considered an excellent imitation of an airline captain. "I've brought you some g-goodies."

The two women looked at each other. Lindy shook her head.

"We don't want any of your 'goodies' Captain," Lindy called out. "What we want is to be off this boat and back with our husbands."

"I'm af-afraid that's beyond my con-control. But listen, I really do have some nice app-appetizers pr-prepared by our chef, and a coup-couple of bot-bottles of some excellent wine."

"Captain, just go away," Lindy said. She looked at Pam and whispered, "He's loaded."

"I won't st-stay long."

"Leave us alone!" Pam cried.

They heard a scrapping noise on the door as the captain fumbled around trying to insert the key in the look. With a click, the door opened. The captain stood in the middle of the doorway, a key in one hand, two bottles of wine in the other and a tray of hors d'oeuvres was on the floor by his feet. Lindy took a few quick steps to shut the door in his face, but the captain put out his arm. He held the door open, slid the tray in with one foot then entered the cabin. He closed and locked the door.

Lindy and Pam backed as far as they could into the cabin.

The captain smiled. "Now listen, don't go and get yourselves all up-upset. I thought may-maybe the three of us could have ourselves a little par-party."

"Leave us alone!" Pam cried. Her body shook and tears welled in her panicked eyes.

"Look, this'll be such a good time! I prom-promise!"

He felt for the light control to dim the room.

"That's much better. Now, while I op-open the wine, you can de-decide which of you is gonna get un-undressed first," he laughed. "Oh, this is gonna be great fun!"

Lindy frantically looked around the room for something with which to club the captain.

The captain managed, after several inept attempts, to remove the cork from one of the bottles. He poured a glass for himself, took a large gulp and declared it to be, "Good stuff! You can have some. So, what did you girls decide? Who's up first?"

"You're disgusting! Get out of here, now!" Lindy shouted.

The captain laughed, then slurped down the rest of the wine in his glass.

His demeanor shifted in a split second. His face changed from a silly, drunken smile, to a grotesque leer. His voice now more of a guttural growl. "I'm trying to be nice, I wa-wanna be nice, but if you two bitches can't decide, I'll do it for you! Now, let me see . . . ." With his lust glazed bloodshot eyes, he stared from one to the other.

"Don't you dare take a—" Lindy started to scream just as the captain lurched toward Pam. Pam quickly side stepped the captain. Narrowly missing her, he banged into a night stand.

He turned back to face them, his cheeks flushed crimson.

His laugh was insidious.

"Oh, this really is f-fun," he snarled, lunging at Pam and again narrowly missing her. This time he stumbled onto one of the beds.

Taking advantage of the moment, Lindy grabbed a wine bottle off the cart. Holding it by the neck, she rushed the captain. She swung the bottle at his head, but turning quickly, he caught her arm in mid-swing. As they struggled for control of the bottle, the captain brutally backhanded Lindy across the face with his free hand. Lindy tumbled to the floor, her mouth bleeding, the bottle rolling out of her hand.

"Enough of this bu-bull-shit," he growled, his face a mask of lust and anger. He began to unbuckle his belt. "This par-party is about to begin!"

His pants had slid down by his knees just as the cabin door was flung open. Ginger stood in the doorway, a pistol pointed directly at the captain.

"Sorry, Captain, no party. Like, it's over. Ya know what I mean?"

While giving Ginger a venomous look, the captain attempted to pull up his pants.

"You for-for-get who's the captain of this ship? I'm commanding you to give me that gun! Now!"

"No sir, Captain." She kept the gun trained on him and reached into her pocket for her cell phone.

She held the phone in one outstretched hand, and the gun in the other hand.

"Now," she said, pointing the pistol at the captain's groin, "like do I pull the trigger, or do I speed dial Tio?" She paused. A quizzical expression crossed her face. "Like, do I pull the trigger, or do I, like, speed dial Tio? Ya know what I mean? Hmmm. What do you think ladies?"

"Ah, shit Ginger," the captain broke in, "give me a break and put the damn gun away. I had a little too much to drink. I wouldn't hurt anyone, you know that. I was just trying to have some fun."

"Really, what do you call this?" Lindy said, wiping blood from her mouth.

The captain had no response.

"Captain, finish pulling your pants back up and, like, get the hell right out of here before I do something with one of these," she said, looking at her still outstretched hands.

It was almost comical, watching him do as he was told. He kept attempting to pull his pants up as he shuffled toward the doorway.

"I'm really sorry about this," Ginger said. "Every once in awhile he goes off the deep end, ya know? I better talk to Tio again about him, this isn't the first time something like this has happened."

"Thank you, Ginger, thank you," Lindy paused and let out a deep breath. "You saved us. I don't know what else to say. Who is Tio?"

"Oh no, please forget I mentioned him! I shouldn't have done that! Like, I'll be in big trouble! Please forget I said it!"

"Well, we owe you that much," Lindy said.

"One other thing," Ginger said. "The crew's got a poker game going on, and, like, there's a lot of drinking. I think I should spend the night in here with you and the pistol, ya know what I mean?"

"I think that's a good idea," Lindy said, heading for the bathroom to check her bleeding.

"It's stopped . . . no loose teeth . . . guess I'll survive," she called out.

Pam sat on the edge of her bed, her head in her hands, crying again. "I just can't take anymore of this," she sobbed. "Where's Mike? Why hasn't he found me? It's been hours!"

"Okay ladies," Lindy said, in an effort to lighten things up, "our captain has delivered, in a rather unorthodox manner mind you, some finger food and two bottles of wine. I suggest we take full advantage of his stupid hospitality."

Pam wasn't buying into Lindy's mood change. She looked up from the bed, her face red and splotchy.

"Just hand me one of the bottles," she said.

❧

That same night, back on Holden Beach, Tommy Lee and Willy were over at Chief Everhart's. There wasn't not much discussion going on. Each man was nursing a bottle of beer, hoping for one of their phones to ring.

"This isn't right," said Tommy Lee, "just hanging around here while they're in trouble in Miami. It just isn't right, damn it."

"I agree," said Willy, "we ought-a be down there with 'em." He had repeated this several times.

"Hey, this isn't any easier for me than for you two, but they asked us to stay put in case something happens at this end," Curt said. "We have to go by what they think. Damn it now, we just have to sit and wait."

"That doesn't mean I have to like it," Willy said.

❧

That same night, in a sports bar across from La Quinta, Matt and Mike were both nursing a beer. Both men had their hands wrapped around their bottles and were scraping off the wet labels with their thumb nails. There was not much discussion, nor much drinking.

Their phones were atop the bar. They sat, waiting for one of them to ring.

CHAPTER 35

It had taken twenty minutes, not five. But during that entire time, Joan had made no attempt to leave. Mostly, she sat in openmouthed disbelief, often shaking her head in bewilderment. She never took her eyes off Allen as he spoke. He never took his eyes off her fearing she'd bolt and he'd have to chase her down.

"So, that's the 'why' of Miami. You now know about everything there is to know about me, the good, the bad and the ugly. That is, except for the last part."

Joan's eyes were riveted on his. "I don't know whether to get up and slap you, get up and call my brother, or just run out of here as fast as I can!"

"Don't do any of those! Let me finish. I asked you to not leave until you heard the end. The end is the most important part.

Joan, here's the part you must hear before making any decision about me, about us. I need to do everything I can to save those two women. I can't let any harm come to them. This will sound selfish, but I need to do that in order to save myself. I can't blame you if you never want to see me again. I told you I want, I *need* to get away from the kind of life I've lead. I can do that, I *know* I can do it. But I can't start on that path until those two women are safely back with their husbands and I can't do it until I've set some other stuff right. The thing is, I could sure use your help to do this."

"What! You must be out of your mind! You're even crazier that I thought!"

"No, no I'm not. Think about it Joan. You told me earlier that your brother has been trying to nail this creep, Herrera, for a long time. We can do that! And, the only way I can break free from my past is if they can also take down that megalomaniac I still work for.

You make your decision about me, about us, later. The only decision you have to make now is, not whether to leave this table, but whether or not to help save the lives of those two women and get the thugs behind bars. Your decision is whether or not to call your brother right now, so I can work with him . . . *that's* your decision."

♦♦♦

The three of them were in a parking lot around the corner from Joe's Stone Crab, sitting in the captain's cruiser. It was getting dark. Joan had given in to Allen's pleas and called her brother. While they waited for his arrival, Joan became convinced of Allen's sincerity, and that he was being on the level with her in wanting to straighten out his life. She believed his love for her was real, and she knew in her heart, in spite of what she had learned, that she loved him. Now, for the moment, saving the two ladies was paramount in both their lives.

Allen had just finished filling her brother in on the situation.

"So where are they?" Roberto asked.

"I don't know," Allen replied.

"You don't know," the Chief said in disgust. "I oughta haul your ass in right now, you know *that* much, don't you? All you're doing is looking for some kind of redemption for screwing up who knows how many lives over the years."

"Can't say I blame you for thinking that way," Allen said, "but I'm certain I'll be getting a phone call shortly, one with instructions from my boss that will lead to the two women, and, possibly, Tio Herrera."

"Jesus," said Roberto, shaking his head, "*possibly* lead to Herrera."

"Roberto," Joan said, "this could be the opportunity you've been waiting for."

"Or, it could be an opportunity for me to fall flat on my face. Do you realize how much juice this guy Herrera has? If we don't nail him, catch him directly involved, hands on, in the act of something really nasty, it's over for me. The Mayor will have me sweeping sidewalks around Domino Park!"

"Listen," said Allen, "I've gotta talk to the two husbands and let them know something's in the works. If—"

His cell phone rang. He looked down at the caller ID, then looked at Joan and her brother and turned a thumbs up.

For the next several minutes, Allen listened, said "uh huh," repeatedly and nodded his head.

"Got it, Jock, yes, yes, Jock, I got it all," he said, then closed his cell.

"It's on," he said.

"Where are the women?" Roberto asked.

"Give me a minute, Chief. First let me explain that I'm to get the realtor in North Carolina to write up the offer on the property I told you about, then have him fly here and give it to me. Once I make those arrangements, I'm to call Jock, who will arrange to fly here, with the money, in his private jet. I'm also to make arrangements for a chartered yacht out of Fort Lauderdale. So, the timing depends on a few things, but it could all happen as soon as tomorrow, certainly within two days.

"So, where are the women?" Joan asked.

"They must be on a boat, and that boat must be somewhere off the South Florida coast. Or, I suppose, it could be docked somewhere. I don't know, but Jock said we'd need the charter to meet up with Herrera."

"Somewhere off the coast or docked somewhere," Roberto muttered. "Well, shit, that narrows it down."

Roberto paused, and remained silent for several moments before speaking again. "I can tell you this: Herrera is very, very proud of his yacht. He's constantly boasting about it. I'd be surprised if he'd go along with something like this, but you never know. Even those with huge egos screw up occasionally."

"My boss, D'Agostino," Allen said. "He'd do it for him, and expect something in return. That's the way it works."

"Damn, we don't have much time," Roberto said. "Our best chance would be to put together some kind of a sting operation that we can record. But that takes time, and that's something we have little of. The next thing is an insider. It can't work without one. We need someone both Herrera and, what's his name, D'Agostino trust."

"You know you're looking at him," Allen said.

"Allen, as often as not, a sting goes sour. And when it does, somebody gets hurt, really hurt," Roberto said.

"I have a lot of bad stuff to make up for Roberto, and a lot to prove to someone," Allen said, looking at Joan.

Roberto went silent again, the wheels turning in his head.

"With some help, we can locate the boat," he said. "If it's docked, it's a simple all points routine search, and if it's off-shore, the Governor can help us."

"The Governor?" Joan asked, surprised.

"The governor of the state," Roberto explained, "is in charge of the Air National Guard, unless the feds have it mobilized. As I recall, one of their missions in life concerns search and rescue operations. This might be something of a stretch, but isn't that what we're trying to do?"

"Sounds like it's in the line of duty to me," Allen said.

"But why—" Joan started to ask.

"He owes me a favor."

"It must be a pretty big one," Allen said.

"Huge," smiled Roberto.

"Can you elaborate?" Joan asked.

"Only to tell you that it's juicy, really juicy," Roberto laughed.

"Listen, there's a lot to do," he continued. "Allen, after you get Joan home, go see the two husbands. Tell them we're working on something. Be careful, they'll probably want to beat the crap out of you, for which I can't blame them. It's critical that you call me as soon as you know the time table with the flights and all that. You call me immediately. Got it? Here's my card with my emergency cell number."

"Got it."

Joan and Allen traveled back to Joan's place in southwest Miami in silence. Both were thinking about how incredible, on several fronts, the day had been, and about what was about to happen, and the danger involved.

Allen pulled up to the curb in front of her home.

"Allen, please don't get out," Joan said. "I don't know when I'll see you again, or *if* I'll see you again. I can tell you that I love you, but I need, *we* need all this behind us before we go any farther. Please be very, very careful."

Before he could respond, she opened the door and got out of the car.

"I love you too," he whispered into the void.

❦

Driving back to La Quinta, Allen decided it would be best to call Mike first, rather than just show up at his room. Hopefully, that would lessen the possibility of being punched out. He could explain, over the phone, that he was involved in a plan to get the wives back, explain that he was now working on Mike and his buddy's behalf, and that it was critical that he meet with them both.

His reasoning made all kinds of sense. Unfortunately, after talking to Mike, it didn't work out quite the way he had planned.

Allen had no sooner knocked on Mike's door than it flew open. Matt reached out, grabbed Allen by his shirt collar and roughly threw him into the room. As he stumbled forward, Mike grabbed the back of Allen's shirt, stood him up and viciously delivered his tightened fist into Allen's gut, doubling him over.

"You bastard," Mike sneered, as he swung his fist toward Allen's face, cold-cocking him across the chin. Allen crumbled onto the carpet and laid there, not moving.

"Damn it, I didn't mean to knock him out," Mike said, breathing heavily.

"Well, so much for good intentions," Matt said.

After Allen had called Mike earlier, Mike and Matt agreed to stay calm, control themselves, and hear the creep out. It hadn't worked. Seeing Allen, both men's fears and frustrations took charge and the adrenaline kicked in.

"The best laid plans—" Mike said.

Matt went into the bathroom, got the ice bucket, which at this point contained mostly ice water, and dumped it on Allen's face.

Both men watched as Allen came slowly around, looked at them, realized where he was, and held up a hand in surrender.

He shook his head several times and attempted to sit up.

"I can't blame you," he said, rubbing his jaw, still somewhat dazed, "guess I would have done the same thing. I just hope you guys have it out of your system."

"Maybe, but I wouldn't count on it," Mike said.

"I guess that's about as good as I can hope for," Allen said, grabbing the bed spread and pulling himself up. He worked himself into a sitting position, then leaned back against the side of the bed.

"We need to talk," he said.

CHAPTER 36

Roberto, Miami's Police Chief and Joan's brother, met with Allen, Mike and Matt in Allen's room the following afternoon. Allen had not heard back from D'Agostino regarding his boss's flight plans.

"Well, we got a break there," said Roberto, "it buys us some time. With the Gov's help, we've located Herrera's yacht. They keep moving, but basically they're cruising in circles a few miles out, off of South Beach."

Roberto had set his briefcase on the hotel room desk, and now he opened it. The others gathered around the desk. Inside the briefcase was a complete set-up to "wire" one of the three men. There was also a pen, a gun and a holster.

"You've each seen wires used on about every damn show on TV, so I don't have to explain what they're about, but have any of you guys seen one of these?" He held up the pen.

"Well, I'll bite," said Matt, "and take a wild guess. It's a pen."

The others laughed nervously.

"You're absolutely right," said Roberto, "but, gentlemen, it's much, much more." He pushed a barely noticeable button on the pen and clipped it inside his shirt pocket.

"It looks like a pen, it writes like a pen, but this little baby, at this very moment, is recording our meeting. It is recording the sound along with video in living color. No wires, no plugs, no cables. It'll run for over ten hours just on the battery. He removed the pen from his shirt pocket, shut it off, and handed it to Matt.

"Really amazing," he said, turning the pen in his hand, "so why do we need the wire?"

"The pen doesn't transmit, it only records. We need to transmit to the police boat so we know when to move in."

"Oh, right," said Matt.

"Listen gentlemen, and listen well. I can't over emphasize how dangerous this operation is going to be. The truth is, we couldn't figure out any other way to pull this off. Herrera is a bastard, he's as mean as they come. I don't know about this D'Agostino guy, but my guess is he's cut from the same cloth. Lives are at stake. Yours, as well as the others. I need to know now if you each are in."

The room was silent.

"I can't think of any other way to get our wives back," said Mike.

"There is another way," said Matt, looking over at Mike. "You accept D'Agostino's offer. It's as simple as that. He hands over Pam and Lindy, and, I guess, the money, and we go back home."

"I'm afraid it's a little too late for that," Roberto said. "We now have the governor of the state involved, the Air National Guard involved, and, because it's a kidnapping, we'll have an FBI agent on board to make certain everything goes down properly so the bad guys can be successfully prosecuted."

"Damn," said Mike, "I really screwed up."

"No, you didn't," said Roberto. "If this goes as planned, and there's no reason why it shouldn't, your wives will be safely back with you, and, at a minimum, two of the most dangerous criminals in this country will be going away for a long time, hopefully, for the rest of their lives."

"For Christ's sake man, don't you get it?" screamed Mike. "Our wives could be killed! I don't give a rat's ass about those scum bags you're trying to nail, all we care about is our wives!"

"Hey Mike, back off! I clearly understand," said Roberto, "and we're taking every precaution to make sure that doesn't happen!"

"Mike," said Matt, putting his hand on Mike's shoulder, "we can't start second guessing ourselves at this point or we'll go nuts and really screw things up." He turned and looked back at the briefcase. "Chief, why the gun?"

Roberto was silent for a moment. "I'm sticking my neck way out on this. It could be the stupidest damn thing I've done in my career, and it could cost me my job, but I can't send you in there unarmed. Allen, those guys have no reason to be suspicious of you at this point?"

"None, just the opposite. I'm finally putting this thing together for my boss."

"Okay, so they'd have no reason to frisk you. Actually, even if they did, it wouldn't be out of character for you to be carrying."

"Right."

"Okay, we have a Smith and Wesson revolver with a leg holster. The revolver is small, it's quick and it's uncomplicated. You have five shots. You draw, you fire, simple as that. Hopefully, there will be no need to use it."

"Allen, it wouldn't be unusual for you to have a pen on you, right?"

"Not in the least, I'm seldom without one."

The chief walked Allen through the pen's operation.

"Well, for the same reasons, it'd be best if you wear the wire."

"Looks like my lucky day," Allen said with a nervous laugh. "Isn't this what they refer to as a 'trifecta?'"

Matt and Mike watched as Roberto walked Allen through each piece of equipment.

"Any questions?" he asked, closing the briefcase.

"You sure," said Mike, "there's no chance of me just going out there and signing the papers and getting Pam and Lindy back and forgetting about all this other stuff? At this point, I could care less about the money."

"We're too far along, Mike," the chief said. "They'd know something was up."

Mike ran his fingers through his hair. "All this because I was so damn stubborn! Pam was right. I should have sold. None of this would've happened. I'll never forgive myself if anything goes wrong."

"Mike," Matt said, "we're gonna make this happen. It's going to work. In a few days we'll be back in North Carolina having a beer and bragging to everyone who will listen about how brave we were. We'll be heroes. Hell, they'll probably throw a parade for us in Varnamtown!"

Mike shook his head. "Matt, you are something else, but keep the bullshit up. I'm gonna need it to get through this."

The two friends looked each other, stuck out their hands, and shook. They turned and faced the chief and Allen.

"Let's go get our ladies, then kill the bastards who did this," Mike said.

❦

It came together quicker than expected. Roberto had finalized the plan with the three men and was preparing to leave the hotel room when Allen's cell rang. It was Jock.

Allen listened, said, "Got it," and hung up.

"Tomorrow, late afternoon." he said to the group. "He's flying into Miami's Executive Terminal in the early afternoon and bringing the money in cash. Why, I'm not sure. My guess would be it's coming from someplace off the books. Herrera is picking him up. I'm meeting the realtor at the airport in the morning, getting the paper work, checking it over, and sending his sorry ass back to North Carolina. In the afternoon the three of us will settle in on the boat I'm arranging for and wait for further instructions. That's it guys. What do you think?" he said, looking at Roberto.

"I'd like a little more time, but we're okay."

"Just out of curiosity," Matt said, "when this is over, what happens with all that cash?"

"Honestly, I don't know," Roberto said. "Who it'll actually belong to could be problematical. Most likely it'll get hung up in the courts."

Roberto looked at the three men. "Everybody okay now?" he asked. "Remember, we'll be listening to everything that's going on. The second we hear the deal's gone down, we move in. We'll have the audio from the wire, but Allen, the pen is critical. Hang onto it under any circumstances."

"Only if these two guys promise to let me be in their parade," he grinned.

"Allen," said Matt, "we pull this thing off and you can *lead* the damn parade!"

"Okay, okay," Roberto said. "Let's everyone get a good night's sleep and be sharp for tomorrow."

"You gotta be kidding," Mike said. "Sleep? How in the hell can I get any sleep knowing Pam's out there with those creeps?"

"Mike, Lindy won't let anything happen to Pam. Trust me, she can be one very tough lady," Matt said.

CHAPTER 37

Everything went according to plan. Allen received the paperwork from Billy Bodean at the Miami airport and sent him back on his way. He then finalized the arrangements for a charter out of Fort Lauderdale and received instructions from Jock on where to meet up with Herrera's yacht later that day.

Allen chose to wear a dark brown guayabera. It was loose fitting and concealed the wire. The shirt pocket was perfect for the spy/pen and the Smith and Wesson was strapped to his right leg under his khakis. He felt like 007.

When the three had boarded Herrera's yacht, Matt and Mike were patted down. Allen, as expected, was not.

"You look like a native wearing that thing," Jock said when he saw Allen in the guayabera.

"Hey Jock, you gotta get some of these," Allen replied, "they're the most comfortable damn shirts I've ever worn."

"Well, when we wrap this up let's you and me do a little shopping in Miami," Jock laughed, "we'll start a new fuckin' fashion trend in Chicago!"

Allen, walking alongside Jock, watched as Matt and Mike, both of whom had remained silent, were steered at gunpoint by Herrera into the luxurious salon of the yacht.

"Let's get this done real quick," Herrera said, "I'm getting more than a little antsy about this whole damn operation. Allen, get the paperwork signed, then get everyone the hell off of my yacht."

"Listen," said Mike, "you can give all the damn orders you want, but I ain't signing a damn thing 'til we see our wives."

"You sign off on the deal, then you get the women," Jock said.

"Bullshit," said Matt. "Nothing happens, nothing at all, 'til our wives are here with us."

Jock hesitated, then looked over at Herrera and nodded.

Herrera left the salon as Jock drew a revolver from his jacket.

Pam was the first to enter the salon, and, seeing Mike, rushed into his arms. Lindy followed, and was quickly embraced by Matt.

There were hugs and tears.

"Okay, okay, the reunion is over folks," said Jock, impatiently. "You," he said, pointing the revolver at Mike, "get over to the desk with Allen and sign the damn papers. Make it quick!"

Matt put an arm around Pam as Mike left her side.

When Allen and Mike were seated at the desk, Matt turned to Jock. "Where's the money?"

"Listen asshole, you're just extra baggage as far as I'm concerned. It'd be best for you to just keep your fucking mouth shut."

Looking up from the desk, Mike said, "No, he's right, let's see the money."

"Ya know," said Jock, "you're most fortunate that I want your property. Normally I wouldn't take this kind of shit from anyone. I'm trying real hard to be nice, but believe me, it's wearing thin."

He left the salon and returned shortly carrying a large, black leather case which he placed on the gaming table. He removed a key from his pocket and opened the case. Mike and Matt walked over to the table. Inside the case were stacks of one hundred dollar bills.

"My god," Mike said under his breath.

"Better than shrimpin' for a fuckin' living, eh?" Jock said.

Jock closed the case. Allen, sitting at the desk, had turned to "watch" the scene at the game table, and was back to studying the papers. He now had all the video he needed. He walked Mike through the papers, instructing him where to sign.

Allen, Mike and Matt, were each wondering the same thing. They had the video of the women being returned, proving a kidnapping had taken place. *Where the hell were the cops*?

The deal, for all intent and purposes, had been completed when Tio Pipo Herrera looked over at Allen and casually asked, "Allen, I noticed you took a pen from the desk drawer to sign the papers. Is something wrong with yours?"

"No, nothing, it works just fine, Tio," Allen replied, a bolt of fear shooting through his chest. Allen looked down at the pocket. "I forgot I had it on me."

"Really," Herrera said, "a lawyer forgetting his pen, that's strange." He swung his pistol toward Allen. "Jock, check out Allen's pen."

"Tio, are you kidding me? Allen's my main man!"

"Humor me, Jock. My apologies ahead of time if everything's on the up and up."

Jock walked over to the desk and removed the pen from Allen's pocket. "Sorry," he said to Allen.

He turned the pen around in his fingers studying it, then leaned over the desk and scribbled on a piece of paper.

"Works fine, Tio. Wait . . . what the hell's that!" He was staring at the pen. "Holy shit!" He had spotted something that triggered his alarm, most likely, the lens.

"Get up, damn it," he commanded gruffly, "and turn around!"

He grabbed Allen's shoulder and spun him around. He patted Allen's back, then jerked up his shirt.

"You son-of-a-bitch! You rotten son-of-a-bitch!" he screamed in disbelief. "The fucker's wired, Tio! The two-timing bastard is wired! I should rip your fucking head off!" he screamed as he swung his pistol at the base of Allen's skull. Allen collapsed to the floor. Jock leaned down and tore open the back of the guayabera. He grabbed the wire and ripped it off Allen's body. Then he stood up, threw the wire to the floor, smashing it with the heel of his shoe. He next dropped Allen's pen to the floor and again using the heel of his shoe, crushed it.

"God damn it, I should have known better. I didn't like this from the start." Herrera screamed. "We gotta move!"

He grabbed the intercom mike and shouted for the captain to head out to sea, full throttle.

"Sir, there's a boat tethered to us."

"Cut the damn line and move out!"

"Sir, we have a police boat closing in off our starboard! I saw it earlier but thought it was a fishing boat."

"Ah, shit!" Herrera screamed, "open her up anyway!"

"You people," said Jock, "you god damn rednecks," he said waving his gun at all of them.

Allen began to stir. "And you Allen," Jock sneered, looking down, "I don't know what's gonna happen next, but you ain't gonna live to see it. As he took aim at Allen's head, Matt picked up a pillow off the couch and threw it at Jock. It struck Jock hard enough to throw him off balance, but he got a shot off. It hit Allen.

Herrera looked over at Jock. "I can't believe how I let you fuck up my life! You and your fucking 'main man!' I didn't like this shit from the beginning!"

Herrera shook his head, pulled the trigger and shot Jock straight in the heart. Jock crumbled to the floor, his eyes wide, his face a mask of shocked disbelief.

Keeping an eye on the others, he went over to Jock and removed the pistol from the dead man's hand. "Well, maybe I do have a chance after all. You four will be found dead from shots fired from Jock's pistol. I shot Jock with mine while attempting to save you four from his fury. Unfortunately, I was a second too late. I'm certain I can battle incarceration for years, possibly for whatever time I have left on this planet. Funny how things work out."

He had a gun in each hand now, and turned toward Mike.

"Sorry, folks," he said, leveling Jock's gun at Mike.

"Drop it Tio," said a soft quivering voice behind him.

Herrera didn't flinch. "Ginger, is that you?"

"Yes, Tio."

"What are you doing, my love?"

"I can't let you murder these people, okay? It's wrong, okay? It's so very, very wrong, Tio."

"But if I don't—" he spun quickly and fired at Ginger. The shot struck Ginger in her left shoulder, knocking her back. As she fell, she fired off a wild shot that hit Herrera in the arm that was holding Jock's pistol. The pistol fell to floor by Allen. Herrera recovered and reached down. Allen grabbed the pistol just as Herrera put his hand on it. They struggled for the gun. Matt hurried over to help just as another shot rang out. No one moved, then Tio Pipo Herrera, his face, not unlike Jock's, in a look of stunned shock, slumped to the floor.

Lindy rushed over to Ginger's side. She was sitting on the floor, head in hands, crying.

"I loved him, I really, loved him, ya know? He was good to me. But I couldn't let him do it, I just couldn't let him do it, ya know?" Ginger's wound was bleeding profusely.

"Where in the hell are the cops?" hollered Matt.

"They're here," Roberto hollered, rushing into the salon.

"We need a medic!" Lindy screamed.

"Right behind me," Roberto told her.

"My God, what's happened here?" Roberto asked, looking around. "We lost contact when the wire was discovered."

As Matt explained how it all happened, Roberto walked over and looked down at D'Agostino's body, then over to Herrera's.

He walked over to where the medic was working on Ginger. "It's not life threatening," the medic said, "but we should get her to a hospital."

"Brave little lady," Roberto said, patting Ginger on top of her head. "From what I just heard, you saved some lives."

"I just couldn't let him do it, ya know?"

Matt was looking about the salon with a quizzical look on his face.

"What's wrong?" asked Mike.

"Has anyone seen Allen?"

They all shook their heads.

"We know he was shot," said Lindy.

"Check every room," Roberto ordered his men.

When they returned to the salon, he was informed Allen was nowhere to be found.

"I'll be damned," said Roberto, "just when he had me convinced." He shook his head. Disappointment registered on his face.

"There's something else," Matt said.

"What's that?" Roberto asked.

"The money," Matt said. "It's gone."

CHAPTER 38

They were seated in the upper level of the Paradise Cafe, where it had all begun.

Of course, by now, everyone on the beach and in Varnamtown had heard about the extraordinary Miami adventure that the four had survived. *The Brunswick Beacon* had even given the story front-page coverage. Although there was no parade, none of the four could leave their home without having to repeat, or clarify, certain aspects of the story.

"To honor our local celebrities," Chris, the Cafe's owner, said, placing three bottles of wine on the table.

"My goodness," said Lindy, clapping her hands. "I could get used to this! We're going to have to get ourselves into more jams!"

"We've already had our fair share," Matt said, picking up two bottles, then walking around the table filling glasses.

The two couples now got together frequently, occasionally included Willy, and had developed a strong bond. The excuse for tonight's dinner was to discuss the christening party for the rebuilt *Naughty Nina*. With good luck and good weather, she'd be back in the water in a month or so.

With the Miami experience behind them, as well as their earlier ordeal in New York City, Mike and Pam joked they'd never leave Brunswick County again.

Matt sat down after pouring the wine, just as Mike was, on a more serious note, explaining his feelings to Lindy.

"Ya know, up until the trouble came, we were really enjoying Miami, and I can understand why you guys like it so much. But, *this* is Pam and me," he said pointing out to the ocean with his wine glass. "That water out there, the marshes, our friends, and *Naughty.* There's nothing more in life we could ask for. It's all right here."

"Well, he's speaking for himself!" interrupted Pam, "a sports car, convertible of course, would really complete the beautiful picture he just painted, don't you think?"

Mike had already told Matt that he'd arranged for just such a car, and would present it to Pam the day the rebuilt *Naughty* was launched.

Mike turned to Matt, still on a serious note. "Listen," he said, "I know we shrimpers and the other fishermen have a ton of problems to face with imports and regulations and competition and all that, but we've got some things working for us, so don't anyone hold a wake for us yet. I'm gonna keep shrimpin'. Now, on another subject, have you talked to our favorite cop lately?"

"Spoke with him yesterday," Matt said. "He's retiring next month."

"What?" exclaimed Mike.

"Yup, seems since his stroke he's learned to appreciate the life of leisure. He's spending a lot of time hanging out at the fishing pier and has made some fishing buddies there. He's read several books he's enjoyed and I've had him out crabbing."

"That's great, good for him."

"And Maria and Carlos?" Pam asked.

"They're doing just fine. Still don't know about their permanency in this country, but he's happy working for that painter in Myrtle Beach. He's making enough for them to have their own trailer, and the baby is doing great."

"You should have seen the look on Tommy Lee's face when Carlos told him they had named the baby Tomás," said Lindy. "He actually cried. Oh, and don't let me forget Matt, we have to bring them up for *Naughty's* christening."

"Speaking of the christening," said Mike," raising his glass to Willy, "you and Tommy Lee have done an incredible job with *Naughty . . .* thanks partner."

Mike and Willy clicked glasses. "Tommy Lee was a big help," he said, "no two ways about it. So, what's the latest on Billy Bodean?"

"That's sorta up to me Willy," Mike said. "He and Allen were responsible for the fire, no doubt about that, but neither was involved in the kidnapping in Miami. I have to decide if I want to press charges. To tell you the truth, what we really want is to just get the whole mess behind us. But no matter what, he's finished around here. He'll most likely pack up and move from the area."

"Well, good riddance is all I can say; he was a bad man. While we're talking about it, you just mentioned that Allen guy. Did you ever hear any more about him or the money?"

"Nothing," said Matt.

The timing of this conversation was just short of incredible.

Willy, sipping his wine and wishing it was beer, looked toward the stairway.

"Well, I'll be darned," he said, "remember that insurance fella I told you was asking about Mike when y'all were in Miami? That's him over on the stairs."

All heads looked over to the stairway.

"It can't be," said Mike.

"No, I don't believe it," said Matt.

At the top of the stairway, dressed in his patented oxford shirt, khakis and loafers, stood Allen Skubic. He was smiling from ear-to-ear as he approached their table.

He looked straight at Mike. "Your neighbor told me you

might be here."

Everyone at the table was speechless.

Matt was the first to recover. "Allen, my god, I don't whether to call the cops, punch you out, or get up and give you a hug!"

"I'll take the hug," Allen laughed, "no need for the cops. I'm not a fugitive, well, not in Florida, anyway, and I hope not here. Believe me, I've got a lot to tell you."

"And you believe me, we're all ears," Matt said. "Grab a chair, have some wine, and start talking."

"I do have a lot of explaining to do, don't I? I hope, after you hear me out, you'll sorta let me off the hook on that, ah, well, that situation I was allegedly involved in with one Mr. Billy Bodean Dudley." He looked at Mike again.

"Something tells me we're about to hear the greatest story ever told, or something close to it," Mike said. Actually due to his role in getting the women safely back, Mike had already decided not to press any charges against Allen. Billy Bodean was the lucky recipient of Mike's thinking. If Mike went after Billy Bodean, then Allen would be dragged into it.

"Okay," Allen said, "before I get to the serious stuff, I'd like to return this package to the lady who dropped it along Lincoln Road in Miami." Allen reached into his shirt pocket, removed a plastic bag, and handed it to Lindy.

"Oh, my God! These are the cigars I bought for Matt! How did you—"

"Don't ask," laughed Allen. "I'm not too proud of what happened that day."

"My goodness. Well, this is very nice of you," Lindy said, and handed the cigars to Matt.

"Okay, second on my things to cover with you good people, and as a consequence of the Florida, ah, situation, I found the girl of my dreams and am crazy in love."

The group's reaction was one of disappointment. Allen's love life was not at the top of their interest list.

"That's really nice Allen," Lindy said, "and we're happy for you, but—"

"I met her at one of your favorite restaurants in Miami. She's Cuban, she's smart and she's the most beautiful girl in the world."

"Well, Cuban, *that's* certainly a step in the right direction!" laughed Lindy. "Still—"

"Wait! This is important. I was falling in love with this beautiful creature before I knew this, but, as it turns out, my future brother-in-law is Miami's top cop, the Chief of Police."

"Roberto? *Our* Roberto?" Mike gasped. "I don't believe it. You and his sister are going to get married?"

"Wow, now it really does get interesting!" exclaimed Pam.

"Does Roberto know this?" asked Lindy.

"Yup, and he approves, as does the rest of the family. We're getting married next month and you are all invited to the wedding."

"Yea!" Lindy hollered, raising her glass, "another trip to Miami! Yippee! Hey folks,"she said, looking around the table, "I'm beginning to really like this guy!"

"Okay," Allen said, "there's more good news."

"Betcha this is about the money," Willy said.

"It is."

"Listen," said Mike "before you get to that, we really want to know just how in the hell you got away."

"Well, the money and the get-away are sorta tied together."

"Hold on," Willy said. He waved to the waitress. "Hon, a bottle of Bud here, and these guys are gonna need more wine, lots more."

"Okay, here's the deal," Allen said. "Things in the salon got pretty chaotic as you'll recall. D'Agostino's shot just grazed my head, thanks to the pillow that Matt threw. I bled alot, but the shot barely hit me. I hugged the floor listening to everything. I almost got up when Herrera shot D'Agostino, but thought it might help later if Herrera thought I was still out of it. During the whole time I was down, I kept thinking about the money. Then I had the scuffle with Herrera for the gun and even after that, I kept thinking about the money. It was driving me nuts! What would happen to it? Remember when we were in La Quinta with Roberto, making our plans?"

Matt and Mike nodded.

"Roberto said," Allen continued, "that what happens to the money could be problematical. He didn't know. I'm laying there thinking it could go back to D'Agostino's family, it could remain in police lock-up for years, there could be a lengthy court battle, yada, yada, yada. Then it hit me! Think back. I was on my feet by then, but the cops and medics were busy with Herrera's and D'Agostino's bodies, looking after Ginger, talking to the crew and you guys, etc. The game table was close to the doorway. I looked around, saw no one was paying any attention to me, picked up the case and walked out! It was so simple! When I got topside, I saw the police boat tethered to the yacht with no one in it. The only person topside was the yacht's captain. A stack of hundred dollar bills from the case took quick care of him. He looked the other way as I left in the boat I had chartered."

"Damn lucky," said Matt.

"Timing and money are everything," Allen replied, "well, not quite *everything.*"

"Where'd you go?" asked Pam.

"Take a wild guess."

"Your-bride-to-be," said Pam.

"Yup! I got to her place, told her everything that had happened and why I took the money and asked her to call Roberto. He came over as soon as he could. Because of my part in the rescue operation, he didn't see how I could be charged with anything, certainly nothing that would stick. And, of course, he knew about me and his sister at that point. So, leaving the scene was not a problem, but—"

"But, the money was," interrupted Mike.

"So where's the money!" shrieked Pam and Lindy at the same time.

"I never told Roberto I had taken it. Remember, no one saw me. But, he knows. I reminded him of what he'd said about it being a problem. Then I presented him with a purely theoretical scenario. Suppose, for example, whoever had the money deposited it in an off-shore account. And say that account would be managed by three people and the only way any money could be withdrawn was for good and noble causes that all three must agree upon. Not a dime could be used for personal purposes or personal gain.

At first he must have thought I was crazy, but he didn't say a word. Then he said, if they were honest and good people, that such a scenario, although far fetched, was possible. He said he'd like to hear, off and on, on how much good was being done. After that, he never said another word."

"So, the money is in an off-shore account with three people having access. And those three must agree on its use?" asked Matt.

"Yup, and before we go any farther, it really gets confidential at this point."

Mike realized why Allen made that comment. "Willy is family, Allen."

Everyone, including Willie, nodded their head.

"Good enough." Allen took out his wallet and removed two slips of paper. He handed one to Matt and one to Mike.

"The phone number and account number are on there, along with three code names."

Mike looked down at his slip. Below the numbers, three names were listed:

Shrimp Boy

Crabby

Mojito Man

"I'll let you guess as to who is who," he laughed.

"I don't know," Mike said, "let me get this straight because I just don't feel—"

"Wait, Mike," Lindy said, butting in, "the money can only be used for worthy causes that you three men agree on, right?"

"Right, that's the stipulation."

"Okay, let me try a for-instance. I know a brave young lady, like who deserves a break in life, ya know, and who, like, could get a whole new life if she had the opportunity of a college education. Ya know what I mean?"

"Ginger!" Pam shouted.

"Perfect," said Allen, "just perfect."

"Okay, here's another one," Pam said. "We know this fella who can't afford to repair his shrimp boat and therefore can't earn a living and—"

"Jimbo!" Matt exclaimed.

"Sounds to me that you guys are definitely on the right track," Allen said.

"And it sounds to me as though we have a couple of very compassionate advisors," said Matt.

"Still," Mike said, shaking his head.

"Mike, think of all the good that can be done," said Pam. "There's the family assistance program for all those people who are really in need, there's the literacy group in Brunswick County teaching people how to read, there's the—"

Okay, okay, okay," said Mike, shaking his head, "enough, I'm sold."

"I have no intention of touching the fund," Allen said. "I just need to be kept in the loop and every once in awhile I'll report to Roberto on how wise the decision was to ignore the missing money. The only other suggestion I have is that everything you do should be anonymous."

"Right," said Matt. "We should have a lawyer, hopefully pro bono, handle the actual transactions."

The table grew quiet. There was much to absorb.

"Listen," Allen said, "I lucked out in getting to you guys so quickly. I'm gonna try to catch a late flight back to Miami. Now, please, I'm serious about the wedding. You have to meet my lady. And Mike, I'd consider it an honor if you would be my best man. I never would have met Joan if you hadn't stuck to your convictions and refused to sell."

Mike looked up and meet Allen's eyes. They stared at each other for a brief couple of seconds. "Absolutely," he said, "it would be an honor."

Matt picked up his glass, "I'd like to propose a toast."

They raised their wine glasses and Willy raised his bottle of Bud.

"I'd like to propose a toast to the bravest little lady any of us have ever met," he raised his glass higher . . . "to Ginger!"

"To Ginger!" they shouted.

Allen got up to leave. "This has really been incredible," he said. He walked around the table shaking hands with the men and embracing the ladies.

"Wait," said Lindy, "you and your bride can come up for the christening of *Naughty*. You can honeymoon here."

"Well, er, Joan has already planned on Spain, but we won't miss the christening, I promise."

"Joan?" Lindy asked, "I thought you said she was Cuban."

"Believe me, she is, but it's a long story. Lindy, I know you're going to love her. Now, I've gotta run. I'll send you the wedding info and see you all in Miami." he said, turning toward the stairway.

"Hold on a second," said Matt, standing. He again raised his glass. "There's one more toast in order."

He looked around the table, then to Allen.

"To a man who laid his life on the line for us, to a man we now call our good friend . . . to Allen!"

Everyone at the table stood and raised his glass.

"To Allen!" they exclaimed.

Allen grinned, shook his head in embarrassment, waved, then quickly headed back to the stairway. He didn't want anyone to notice the tears welling in his eyes.

CHAPTER 39

They were sitting in rockers on the front porch. It was a quiet, crisp late afternoon and they could already tell they were in for a gorgeous sunset over the waterway. When they had first retired to Holden Beach, Matt would take pictures of the more spectacular sunsets, but eventually realized that they occur with such frequency that he no longer bothered. There was no need to look at pictures when they experienced the real deal many evenings.

Matt was enjoying a Sapphire martini and Lindy a glass of Chardonnay.

Lindy broke the silence, "Matt?"

"Uh huh."

"I'm worried about Pam and Mike."

"How's that, they seem pretty happy together to me."

"No, no, that's not what I mean. Mike keeps saying it's getting tougher and tougher to make a living shrimping. They can't touch the Florida money, so eventually they could be in trouble."

"Hon, he's doing what he wants to do, it's in his blood. If folks were aware of the deplorable condition under which much of the imported farm seafood is raised, they wouldn't touch the stuff with a ten foot pole. Mike said they're working on getting that message out, so for us not to hold a wake for the good guys just yet."

"I hope he's right. I'm really glad we got to know them."

"Me too, they're a terrific couple."

They each took a sip of their drink and stared out at the waterway.

Lindy again broke the silence.

"We've been awfully lucky so far."

"For sure."

"It's scary. You just never know what's going to happen. We've had some close calls. We have friends and family who are not well, and many who are no longer with us. The farther along we get, the more, well, tentative, the more *fragile* everything seems."

"It is, Hon, that's why we try to enjoy and find some good in each day."

"Hon," Lindy said, picking up her glass, "we've traveled a lot. We've been to a lot of places."

"Sure have. We've been most fortunate."

"Okay, thinking about where we've been, and where we haven't, what would be your perfect Bucket List trip?"

"Wow, that'd be tough. I don't know, hmm, money's no object?"

"Nope. Well, something that wouldn't wipe us out . . . we'd still have to survive afterward."

"What about time? How much time do I have for this dream trip?"

"As long as you like, but be reasonable . . . let's say a month to five weeks."

"Don't know if I could cram it all in." Matt sipped his martini. "This is gonna take some serious thought. Certainly, it would involve Italy. I'd definitely have to see *La Pieta* again."

"You've seen it three times already."

"I still consider it the most incredible work of art ever

created. Hey, is this *my* dream trip, or what?"

"It is, it is. Okay, what next?"

"Well, more time in Italy outside of Rome, possibly Orvieto. We already know the wine there is great."

"Sounds good so far, keep going."

"We catch a Verdi or Puccini opera at La Scala in Milan, then maybe a week along the Almafi coast. We'll have to do some research on that. We can Goog . . ."

"Don't you dare say it! But, are we ever going to leave Italy on this trip?"

"Sure," Matt laughed, "how much time do I have left?"

"About two and a half weeks."

"Okay, you take it from here."

"No, it's your trip. Hey, you know I'll enjoy wherever you want to go, well . . . for the most part I'm sure."

"Okay, you asked for it. Spain. Back to Barcelona and Seville, and Madrid of course . . . and certainly dinner again at *el Botin* . . . and I've always wanted to go to the Canary Islands, I have family there . . . and a couple of days in Lisbon. We've often talked about Normandy and the D-Day beaches. We should do that on this trip. Back to you."

"We've got one hell of a trip going here," Matt replied. "Okay, here's how we cap it off. We fly back to the states in time to catch Dave Brubeck at the Newport Jazz Festival. He plays it every year. If we can't see him there, we'll find out where he is and go there!"

"Well," said Lindy, "of course the trip won't work out exactly like we want, but we'll come as close as we can."

"Hey, this is a dream trip, right?"

"Right."

They both were gazing down the waterway to a now truly spectacular, orange sunset.

The sky, in turn, had transformed the Intracoastal Waterway into a river of flame. It was a stunning, fiery orange and red world. It was the kind of sunset Matt would have photographed once upon a time.

There was a long silence as the two looked out over the waterway. Lindy reached over and took Matt's hand, a single tear ran down her cheek.

"Matt?"

"Yeah, Hon?"

"I love you."

Matt turned to Lindy and said, softly, "I love you too."

"Matt?"

"Yeah, Hon."

"Let's do it . . . the trip, let's do it."

Matt looked over at Lindy again, then returned his gaze to the waterway. "Look out world, here we come?"

She gave his hand a soft squeeze.

"You betcha," she whispered into the sunset, "look out world, here we come."